ROAM THE
WILD COUNTRY

Ella Thorp Ellis

DRAWINGS BY BRET SCHLESINGER

ROAM THE
WILD COUNTRY

ATHENEUM   1967   NEW YORK

For The Quiroga Sisters

Table of Contents

ROAM THE
WILD COUNTRY

Horse Breaking

IT WAS LATE AFTERNOON BEFORE UNCLE EPIFANIO finally told Martin he might go on down to the corral.

"Go," he said casually so that the other ranch hands might not sense his pride and discover the secret. Martin nodded and left the pasture without a word. How could he tell his uncle that it was too late? Every year of his life Martin had dreamed of the glorious day when he would help break his first horse, when he would ride segundo before all the ranch and do a man's work.

He was only thirteen and would be the youngest segundo in the history of the ranch. Still, it was too late. It was not that he was afraid. Martin knew he would do well. He had been trained from birth for

3

just this day. But would he be riding segundo today if it were not for the drought? That was the question, and the problem.

If only Epifanio had called him last year when the pampa was green and lush, before all northern Argentina had become a dust bowl. He looked out over the prairie stretching as far as he could see in every direction. Usually when he did this, he felt as if he were in an ocean with the afternoon wind moving the pampa grass like a tide, a rich tide that nourished the finest horses and sheep in all Argentina, with plenty to spare. But today there was only a mean stubble a few inches high, too little for a hot wind to move or a hungry horse to forage. The premature seeds crackled like firecrackers across the thirsty land. There would be no seed left for next year. Perhaps there would be no herd to graze either, for this was the worst drought in fifty years, and no man dared look ahead.

As Martin walked, dust rose up in clouds so that his path swirled like a small cyclone. He looked through the dust toward the sun, a relentless monster, and toward the shiny black birds tirelessly circling the flat blue sky. "Only the vultures rejoice," he said bitterly. He had heard that vultures had already attacked the herd of their neighbor. They had not even the honor to wait until death.

But what of his honor? Horses were being broken that the Roca Ranch would normally keep another year, so they could be sold early rather than have their tongues thicken with thirst. He owed his early chance to ride segundo to the fact that they must break more horses this year. That was no way to begin. If only he could find some way to save the whole herd, *then* he would be a great gaucho like Epifanio and today would be the beginning of an honorable career.

Epifanio, second in command only to Don Jaime, who owned the ranch, was the domador, the man on the Roca Estancia who broke horses; only one man in ten thousand had the instinct to do this properly. Don Jaime said it was an art.

If the breaking was cruel, it could ruin the spirit of a fine animal and he would be of no more use than a plow horse. On the other hand, if a horse was not taught that man was his master forever, then this horse was a danger to itself, its rider, and the whole herd. This was particularly true of the high-spirited and sensitive Arabian, who was always a leader and therefore must be dependable. The Roca horses would be ridden on ranches and race tracks and on state occasions all over the world. Epifanio had told Martin that a good domador must think like a man and react like an Arabian; and it was also true that a bit of the domador must remain with each horse he broke.

To Martin it seemed that Epifanio thought like a saint and reacted like a stubborn mule. Once he decided something, no one in all Argentina could change his mind.

"In this I am different, for I listen to others," Martin shouted aloud to the dust. Everyone on the ranch said he and his uncle were alike as two peas. Both had the sharp features and haughty silence of the hawk. Both had unexpectedly soft brown eyes. Both were thin and quick as a hungry puma. Martin had heard these things said over and over, but lately there had been one more comment. "The young hawk is a foot taller than the old one!" Martin was generally proud to be like his uncle. He was so proud that he struggled to be silent and strong, though he often wanted to chatter like a parrot. But he was even prouder to be a foot taller than Epifanio!

"And still growing." Martin walked briskly now. he felt better. It was so hot it seemed you were in purgatory. Dust ran in your very blood. But the horse breaking went on. The doma this afternoon would be as it had been for more than a hundred years on the Roca Ranch. Droughts came and went but the life of the ranch and its heart, which was the breaking and training of champion horses, went on. Suddenly Martin felt it always would. He did not know how they would save the horses, but he felt there would be a way. Then his victory today, if he did well, would have meaning. One day he might still be a domador like his uncle. This was the first step, as it had always been.

Now Martin was excited again, as excited as he had always felt he would be when he rode segundo. What a crowd there was down at the corral! Everyone on the whole ranch must be eating the dust of the corral this afternoon. Did they know a new segundo was riding? No, that was not possible. Only Don Jaime and Epifanio knew. The others were just there to think about something other than the drought.

It would be his task to ride close to his uncle, so that in case of an accident he could rescue his uncle and control the wild horse. He and Epifanio had practiced a thousand times, but still there was a chance of disaster. He could suddenly forget everything, and not be able to move. Somebody might scream and frighten the horse. . . . One mistake and the entire ranch would say he was a conceited boy trying to do a man's work. He could hear them now. His thin, dark face was defiant and wistful as he scanned the crowd.

He saw his friend Carlos with his brother, Alonso, who was just back from the University in Buenos Aires and thought he knew everything. They were Don Jaime's sons. *Qué cosa.* It looked as if Don Jaime's entire family would watch the doma: not only the married daughters and sons and their screaming children but the three elderly aunts who had watched a thousand domas and would be very critical.

Martin frowned. This was something he did not like, this careful tradition. He knew it would help his

uncle if he could go into the corral and talk gently
to the horse first, as the Indians did with their animals. But he could not do this because this was not
the way horses were broken in Spain three hundred
years ago. The Indians had discovered a great many
new ways to tame horses, Martin believed, that were
better than some of the old ways. But he could not
convince his uncle or anyone else on Estancia Roca
of this. Don Jaime's aunts would see and judge the
same ceremony they had seen for seventy years,
could have seen for three hundred years. They would
not welcome change. Like most people in Argentina
they believed in fate, and changing the ceremony was
tempting the fates.

He strained to see which horse it would be. He saw
his own mount, Gatito, tied by a post. Epifanio was
astride his black stallion. Epifanio rode only black
stallions and owned half a dozen. But the wild horse
had not been brought down yet. No matter; it would
be a friend. Martin and Carlos took them all out to
pasture every morning and brought them home
every evening.

Here it was! The crowd applauded as two gauchos
led a young golden mare into the corral—one of Martin's favorites. She carried her tail high and arched her
long neck, as she docilely allowed herself to be led
into the corral and admired. She was a small horse,
but deep in the chest, with a short back and level long
hindquarters. The afternoon sun shone brilliantly on

her golden chestnut coat. She looked around out of enormous black eyes, frightened by all the people but trusting still. *"Pobre,"* Martin thought, *"pobre!"* What a stupid custom it was that kept him from comforting that poor mare now. How much easier it would have been for everyone. But no, that would be changing something, and nothing ever changed in Argentina. Not even the weather. Night and day and month after month it burned the land and parched the animals and caked everything with dry mud.

Epifanio nodded to him. Martin started toward the corral. Though Martin only helped his uncle after the horse was used to the bit, it was also traditional for the domador and segundo to enter the corral together. He hoped the horse sensed a friend near. The audience gasped. Martin noticed the old aunts whispering excitedly to each other.

"Hola, Martin! What are you doing?" called Alonso.

"Playing tennis," he called back as his uncle dismounted and raised his arm solemnly.

"We will try a new segundo for the Estancia Roca," Epifanio announced.

"The fledgling hawk is ready to try his wings," Don Jaime said.

"But, he already soars higher without leaving the ground," a gaucho shouted, referring to his height. The crowd laughed.

"Ah, but the soul is truer than the eye, and perhaps

even today we shall see how tall he really is,"
Epifanio retorted.

"A moment of truth! A moment of truth!" the
crowd yelled.

"On his first day, for shame. Have you no patience?" one of the aunts cried.

Martin thanked her with a smile. He did not want
a moment of truth today either, not yet. There was
time for that when he was ready and experienced.
The point where a horse was actually broken and
finally obeyed the domador was considered the moment of truth. It was like the moment of truth in a
bullfight because it was a time when a man finally
understood the extent both of his courage and his
skill. This occurred for the domador every time he
broke a horse, and was why a good domador was re-
spected above all men on an Argentine ranch. But a
moment of truth occurred for a segundo only if there
was some accident that forced him to take over. The
crowd always loved this because everyone knew a
domador would do well, but no one knew if the
segundo had the courage to break a horse—especially
this segundo, Martin thought.

"We do not need a moment of truth to know he is
very tall indeed if he has been trained by his uncle
Epifanio," another aunt added graciously.

"*Hola, hola!*" Everyone applauded this compliment.

Don Jaime held up both arms for silence. "*Basta,*

enough," he said. "We begin."

Epifanio also raised his hand and the crowd became absolutely silent. He lifted the latch to the corral, and he and Martin stepped inside. From this moment no one must say a word. If a baby cried, it must leave. If a man coughed, he must leave. "If a man died, he must do it without a death rattle," was the old saying for the silence required during the breaking of a horse. Any noise would distract the horse, and hours spent winning its confidence would be lost.

Dust settled gradually around them as they stood just inside the corral. There was no breeze now, and the heat was intolerable. Martin was drenched in perspiration, but it gave him no relief. The flies annoyed him, the dust choked him, and the sudden silence oppressed him. How did the mare stand it?

She stood for a moment, sniffing the air, sensing some difference and trying to understand what it might mean for her. She pivoted slowly, seeing first the wide pampa and then the people outside the corral and finally focusing on Martin and his uncle. Epifanio walked a few steps toward her. She caught his scent and shied. She gave a high, frightened whinny. Martin longed to answer as he often did in the pasture. His throat felt dry. She whinnied again and again, high, short, and ever more fearful cries now.

Suddenly she went wild, charging the corral at every point, her nostrils dilated with fury and fear, her long mane like a cloud and her tail held high and switching constantly. She snorted, charging both men and corral. Epifanio and Martin leaped through the blinding dust to the railing.

She galloped round and round the corral, no longer with purpose but crazed with fear. Martin longed to comfort her. She seemed so alone, charging around without another of her kind, while the people stared at her.

An Indian brave trained his horse over a period of months without ever using a corral or a whip or a quirt. He never allowed another human being to watch. He was one with his horse.

Epifanio sat quietly on the railing, waiting. Finally the filly slowed and stood in the middle of the ring, so perfect an Arabian that Martin gasped. He had not realized how beautifully she stood; and even through the dust, the sun reflected on a magnificent golden chestnut coat. There was both fear and pride in her stance. She was waiting to see what fate had in store for her.

Epifanio eased himself from the railing. The mare lay back her ears and curled her lip. But she stayed her ground and let the man make the next move. He clucked his tongue against the roof of his mouth in a call she could understand, a gentle call. He cooed to the horse. He did not go closer, but waited to see if the mare might come to him.

They looked at each other, the man and the horse.

It was a battle of wills, but in the end Epifanio coaxed
her toward him. He placed a carrot between them on
the dirt. With a toss of her delicate head she eased
toward it, nudged it, and the carrot disappeared into
her mouth in three bites. All the while Epifanio talked
softly, telling her of the places they might go together, the strange sights they would see, the fresh
winds they would feel, the fine colts she would surely
bear, and of anything else that came into his mind.
Martin smiled as his uncle described the morning's
milking and the beauty of the dawn over the pampa.

A man coughed! The horse stiffened and laid back
her ears. The fool! He could cough at home in bed
if he had to. What would she do? She neighed, and
Martin's horse, Gatito, answered her this time. Why
had he not answered before? Martin did not know.
She cocked her head. Epifanio cooed. She answered.
Good, she was not frightened. It was all right.

What a beauty! Surely Don Jaime would keep her
for the ranch if all went well this afternoon, if they
did a good job. What a terrible crime it would be if
this horse were ruined during the breaking. Martin
felt sick. So much depended on how well Epifanio
and he did, not only for themselves and Don Jaime
but for the little chestnut mare as well. He felt he
had never *really* known this before, though he had
talked of the responsibility of the domador. He
looked at his slender little uncle and saw that he realized exactly what was at stake. His hands were

clenched and his face tortured as he cooed gently
to the mare.

Now! Epifanio moved imperceptibly toward the
horse. She stood her ground. He held out his hand,
and without moving her hoofs she leaned forward
to sniff it. Her velvet lips fumbled, searching the palm
and the fingers. She wanted to know Epifanio by his
scent, and he was willing. There was not one false
move from either man or horse; the feline grace of
the one was answered with an equal fluid beauty by
the other. They looked as though they were dancing.
It was mesmerizing.

The crowd sighed. Fools! The mare shied and
backed away a few steps. Epifanio seemed not to
notice. He kept talking and did not move his hand
until she nuzzled him again. She looked young to be
broken. Only a two-year-old. They must be breaking
her early because of the drought. Like the seeds and
the meager crops, her breaking must come too soon
because of the drought. Epifanio must be particularly
careful not to break her gentle spirit, because she was
so young. The fierce sun left nothing untouched.

Epifanio was telling the little mare now how he
admired the set of her head and the luminescence of
her eyes; that she would surely be the mother of
champions, a noble horse fit to be the companion of
brave gauchos. He patted her back, running his hand
over her spine. She arched her neck in pleasure.

He held the bridle in his other hand, trailing the

rope in the dirt. He lifted the bridle and slipped it over the golden mare's head in one effortless motion. There was no hurry nor importance given the motion, nor any break in the rhythm of his voice, and the horse scarcely seemed to notice.

The bit hung loose still, and Epifanio eased it into her mouth. She worked her mouth around the alien metal uncomfortably, twisting her jaws in an effort to spit it out. Still Epifanio talked with her, explaining why the bit was necessary and telling her that within a week she would not feel it. She looked at Epifanio reproachfully, whinnied, shied, but did not break loose and run. This was crucial. If a horse objected too strenuously to the bit, the rest of the breaking must be postponed.

She bared her lip and tried to bite. Epifanio stood quietly petting and talking with her. She did not like what had happened, but she was not going to break. Martin looked over at his friend Carlos and smiled. Carlos raised two fingers in a V for victory signal. Epifanio and the mare had passed the first crucial stage.

Epifanio held the bridle while another gaucho slipped in and shackled the mare. This was done within a few seconds, while the horse was still objecting to the bit and before she knew what was happening. Martin wanted to cry out that it wasn't necessary to shackle this gentle one. She could be saddled without the torture of being tied while the saddle was cinched on her back. The Indians didn't shackle their horses. But he knew he could not say anything.

Now Epifanio and the other cowboy virtually threw the saddle on her back. Martin looked full into the horror and betrayal in her eyes. How could they do it? How could Epifanio be so gentle and then betray her? She screamed and bit and tried to roll on the ground, but the men stayed with her and kept cinching the saddle. Within a minute it was secured.

"*Hola!* Remove the shackles," Epifanio called. Martin moved almost automatically to his horse. The ropes were cut, and the man rolled out of the way as the horse charged again in all directions. Many a man had lost his life in this job. Epifanio jumped to a top rung of the corral just beside the gate. He waited while the horse charged and Martin mounted his stallion, Gatito, just outside the corral.

"Open the gates!" As the mare raced through the gates to freedom, Epifanio jumped on her back. In that split second Epifanio proved, as he always did, that he was indeed a domador. His black stallion was saddled in case he missed and had to chase, but he did not miss.

They were off and Martin was right with them, pacing them pitch for pitch as they headed for the open prairie.

"*Caray!*" yelled the old domador at the top of his lungs. "Do your best, little horse" was what he meant. He did not begrudge her spirit and understood how she hated the saddle. This Martin knew. He also knew his uncle enjoyed the wild ride.

"Hear the crowd," Epifanio bellowed at Martin as they headed straight for the prairie. Dimly, as if from another world beyond the dust and the jerking zig-zagging rearing boiling ferment, he heard the people cheering them on.

"They're just letting off steam," he yelled back, and he heard his uncle's laugh.

They headed straight for the open prairie at full gallop, the wild mare whinnying and Gatito answering her. Her mane flew; she carried her tail straight up and her eyes flared defiance. She had been tricked! The pampa was her home, and she would be rid of all encumbrances there. She would be free again!

She galloped effortlessly, her tail flying in the wind she created. Martin and Gatito forced themselves to keep up with her. Within a few minutes Martin felt as if he had been galloping for hours. He'd never be able to keep it up.

But the mare and Epifanio looked as if they could go on rearing and running forever. They were a match for each other. They were nearing the brush now, dangerous land where horses and riders were torn by thorns and bushes and brambles and ripped by unexpected tall branches or spikes. Epifanio had warned him to ride low and protect his eyes. The horse was intelligent, he'd said, and knew this was the spot to throw an unsuspecting man and be on her way.

On they roared, covered by dust that swirled over their heads and obscured the bushes that tore their pants and ripped open their legs and caught in manes and eyes. Sage and cotton were sparse this year, and had more seeds and brambles than ever in an effort to reproduce themselves after a year of drought and uncertainty. Martin felt that he had personally encountered every thorn on the pampa. Would it never end? Wouldn't the sun set, ever?

The mare held to no pattern; there was no figuring her desperate charges first one way and then another. Again and again and again. She was mad to be free. Epifanio was determined to train her. Martin admired both the mare and his uncle. How did they do it?

Round and round they tore through pampa grass and pampa brush, farther and farther from the corral and possible help. The dust rose until the whole sky looked yellow and Martin felt they were enclosed in one horrible cocoon. Men and horses dripped with sweat and were caked with dust.

How long had they ridden? Martin felt with every bone in his body that it had been forever.

Epifanio was singing. Singing! He was absolutely out of his mind.

Suddenly the mare tripped and fell. Epifanio was thrown. Martin lassoed the mare and pulled the rope taut. She would trample her rider if she got the chance.

Where was Epifanio? Over there. He seemed to be sitting up. He must be all right. Dimly Martin heard people yelling. They must have seen what had happened from the corral. They would send help.

Meanwhile the mare reared and kicked and pawed the air while Martin struggled desperately to keep the rope taut as Epifanio had shown him. He had to hold on. He had to keep hold of her until help came and his uncle was safely away. Martin no longer even

thought of whether he was breaking the horse properly or breaking her at all. He was simply keeping her
out of his uncle's way. Tears ran down his face, tears
of frustration and fatigue and fear, but he held on. He
didn't know where he was or even if he was tired.
He simply *had* to keep hold of that rope! The rope
and the dangerous wild horse were all the realities
he knew.

So it was a surprise when he realized they were
slowing down. He felt contrite when he saw that
both the mare and Gatito were foaming at the mouth.
Perhaps he was foaming, too. The wild horse slowed
to a walk and stopped. Martin and Gatito stopped
also. The ground reeled beneath them, and Martin
felt he would fall. Just at this moment he saw that
they were virtually surrounded by people. Everyone
from the corral must be there. What business was it
of theirs? They had not ridden.

"My uncle?" he asked.

"At your service, Segundo," Epifanio replied, and
Martin realized he was standing beside him, offering
to help him from his horse.

"Is it all right? Won't she run away?" he asked in
a daze, pulling the rope taut.

Without a word Epifanio took the rope and walked
toward the shivering horse. She did not move or shy.
He motioned the onlookers to silence. Martin was
stunned. What was Epifanio doing?

The man patted the wild mare. He told her again

all the little flattering tales of what a great mother and companion she would become. He told her she had thrown him as no other horse had done in a dozen years. She should be proud and gracious to a man she had defeated so gallantly, he added softly. At first she shivered with fear and exhaustion, but gradually she responded to the man's gentle touch and finally nuzzled his hand, sniffing strangely at her own scent there.

Suddenly Epifanio leaped from the ground and onto her back in one fluid motion. She reared automatically and then frantically and finally desperately, but he hung on, yelling and encouraging her to do her best, for she would not throw Epifanio Guimenez twice in one afternoon. A few minutes later they were galloping in perfect unison and understanding, as if she had been Epifanio's mount for years.

Epifanio rode the mare back to the corral, leaped from her back, and tied the reins to a post. He was peacefully currying her by the time the rest of the group trudged up.

"I have never seen anything like it," Don Jaime said, voicing everyone's opinion.

"Did I not say the boy would be tall indeed if trained by his uncle," the aunt reminded them as she puffed up.

"Your mare, Patrón," Epifanio said, bowing and handing the reins to Don Jaime, just as if this had been only one more breaking, just as the reins had been handed to the owner by the domador on the Roca Estancia for a hundred years.

"Thank you, Domador. I am in your debt," responded Don Jaime, accepting them.

The spectators clapped and yelled. This had been a doma to remember. Even Martin had never seen Epifanio or anyone else jump on a wild horse's back when the angry animal wore a saddle—and to jump from the ground without using the stirrups—well, it was fantastic!

"And the segundo who rode like a domador—hooray! Hooray!"

Martin blushed as he heard himself cheered. This had, after all, been Epifanio's day, and he was content that it was so. It was hard to understand, though, why Epifanio had not said one word of thanks for keeping the mare out of his way. He expected it, Martin realized suddenly. He expected it! So of course he would never compliment him. That was his uncle! What could you do with a man like that? Martin shook his head and hardly heard Carlos congratulating him.

"Bravo, bravo!" Carlos said.

"The new segundo will train this mare!" Don Jaime shouted above the general tumult. "And you and your uncle must come to the house where we can celebrate tonight," he added.

"Then we must rest before the fiesta," Epifanio said, turning to Martin for the first time since the wild mare had been tamed. "The sky is already red."

It was true. The sunset had thrown a band of scarlet across the sky that reflected back through the pampa so the entire land was red. But there was a coolness now that brought relief after the relentless day. As Martin and his uncle rode silently back across the wide plain to their one room *casita*, the boy felt the vastness of the land that stretched farther than he could see on every side, almost unbroken by houses or fences or trees. He thought of the old saying, "Man's work is no more than a grain of sand in the pampa." Still, what did it require to really please Epifanio? He, Martin, had spent his life trying to please this uncle who had reared him from babyhood, since the day his parents were killed in an automobile accident; and still he was no more than a grain of sand in the vastness of his uncle's thought. He usually satisfied him. Epifanio was rarely angry with him as he was with everyone else on the ranch. But he *never* complimented him. Martin felt he had done well today. Everyone else thought so. Why hadn't Epifanio? Was he clearing his throat to say something?

"Martin," the old domador began. "Martin, I do not want you to think I jumped on the wild mare's back just to show I could ride her. I did not know if I could do it or not, but if she were not broken today there would be no other chance, with all the horses to be broken before next market—because of the drought they must all be sold."

"Even this beauty—they can't!"

"Unless it rains they must."

Martin felt sick. They couldn't sell this horse. If it weren't for the drought they would not consider selling such a superior mare. He *had* to find a way to keep her.

"Martin," his uncle went on, "today, you did well." He said this last very shyly and with pride. But Martin was thinking of the mare and did not hear him. The old gaucho did not repeat what he had said.

The Secret Plan

MARTIN HEARD THE MEN TALKING QUIETLY AS HE walked up the steep horseshoe driveway leading to the Roca Estancia. The jacaranda trees were in full bloom, and blossoms floated around him as he walked. He loved their light perfume. Evening had fallen, and the fireflies twinkled like thousands of fallen stars across the wide valley as far as he could see. It was the time when both the animals who saw by day and those who saw by night were up and about. Birds and viscachas and weasels and snakes were staking out bushes and holes for their rest while the pumas who ruled the night land and the owls who lorded the night skies prowled the lean pampa in search of their breakfast. Martin did not see but felt them all about him and knew the drought had made their hunt a desperate one. "*Pobres, pobres,*" he thought. "We are all but a grain of sand in the life of the pampa."

He heard Epifanio's powerful voice over the general hum of conversation.

"Well, *amigos,* you ask where I learned the trick of jumping a horse as I did today, and only a fool would deny that it's more than a simple trick. Let me give you the long and short of it quickly before Martin comes in, for it was an Indian brave who taught me the skill. And it is no news that Martin thinks the gaucho with a thousand years of Christian experience behind him is no match for the Indian in training a horse."

Oho! So an Indian brave had taught him that trick. Martin decided to wait in the dark and hear the tale.

"If he says what he thinks, he must have inherited the trait," Alonso retorted. Martin had a friend on the terrace.

"Well, we'll not go into that now, though I see the university loosened your tongue, Alonso. To get back to my tale, it took place the year after the last great drought, nearly fifty years ago. Cracks still lay in the pampa big enough to devour an unwary horse or a man, and the great Argentine herds were no more than heaps of bones whitening in the sun and stretching from here north to the Bolivian border. The vultures still circled the skies, though they now drenched the earth with rain, greedy for more than their share.

Some of you will remember those days, for they were blacker than any we've seen since, though God alone knows what's in store for us now. Those were days when a gaucho cinched in his belt and no mistake.

"Anyway, this young brave and I were as close as friends could be. I was newly a segundo then—like Martin, a segundo before my time because of the drought. The Indian boy worked around the ranch and kept his horse alive through the long drought by climbing the few poor trees in the dark of the night and stripping their uppermost leaves for fodder. We each had one poor nag and no prospect of more.

"Then out on the range one day we caught up with a dozen or more wild horses or they caught up with us, depending on how you figure such things. They were beauties, as fat and sleek and frolicsome as if there'd never been a drought. God alone knew how they'd survived, what spring they'd found or fodder they'd eaten, but they were real and no mirage. Well, you can imagine we weren't about to bid them *adiós* when the ranch had scarcely a horse to its name. To say nothing of our hopes of starting a string of horses apiece. And did I remember to tell you that two-thirds of them were black, black as an infidel's heart?

"But how to get them back to the ranch, two lone boys on the wide prairie and a dozen horses free as the wind? I was all for using our boleadoras and whips and riding them down, one on each side, until we came to the ranch, losing whatever we must as we went along. But my friend said no. For he'd observed that the horses were friendly and wanted to play. 'We'll join them,' said he, 'and lead them back like a game. Ride a wild horse apiece and trust our own horses to follow.'

"Ride a wild horse?"

" 'Oh, it's easy,' said he. I thought he was mad, but I was game for any adventure then, so I went along with his plan. We each picked a gentle mare, like the little beauty this afternoon, while the horses were grazing about us, peaceful and secure. He went close and talked with them gently; I followed, and soon they were nuzzling our hands.

"The trick was to jump up and land on the horse's back in an instant, not letting the horse think this was anything special at all, but just in the way of good play. Well, that's what we did, though it's hard to believe, and we galloped on back to the corral without losing a single horse, though I've never recovered from the surprise to this very day."

"And what happened to the Indian boy?" The question hung in the air, for just at this point Martin stepped on a dry branch and announced his arrival. He was furious because now he would never know what had happened to his uncle's Indian friend. He wouldn't dare let on he had been eavesdropping.

"Here is Martin, at last!" Don Jaime announced.

"Sí, we have a cause for rejoicing. Toast your

nephew, Epifanio!"

Epifanio ceremoniously handed Martin a glass and
took one himself. They clicked. "May the segundo
become a domador," he said quietly.

"Bravo!"

"Long live our new segundo!"

"Health, money, and the time to enjoy them!"
One by one the men proposed the traditional toasts,
the toasts they had used and heard used since they
were small children.

Martin choked as the liquid caught in his throat.
Coca Cola! Had he not done a man's work? This
must have been his uncle's idea. Surely Don Jaime
would not deny him wine on this night. He would
drink Coca Cola until he was eighty if Epifanio had
his way. He gave his uncle a furious look but said
nothing. Perhaps the others did not know what he
was drinking.

Martin looked around the eager circle of men
toasting him. Each man wore his black bombacha
pants and full white dress shirt tonight for the celebration. These old friends were glad to have *something* to celebrate, he thought, as he caught the terrible weary acceptance behind the smiles on the taut
sun-baked, wind-etched faces. They were tough men,
men who had given their lives to building the herd.
Some had had herds in the drought Epifanio had
just described, so this was the second herd they might
lose. And they were really afraid they would lose

the whole stock, both sheep and horses, to the drought this year.

But why did such men just accept the drought? Why didn't they try to move the herd to the south where there was water? They didn't lack courage. Half-moon scars gleamed white on the faces of nearly all of them. These were the honorable scars of knife fights, for the gaucho fights to leave this mark and not to kill. And no one in the group had more scars than Epifanio, and no one was more against trying to move the herd.

Why? Because they must obey God's will, they must not tempt the fates, Epifanio would say. He would then point out that Don Jaime's brother had driven the horses south at the time of the last drought, had lost half of them in the ordeal; and then the very next year hail had hit the others, and most had died of the pneumonia that followed. But when he, Martin, pointed out that no one had tried since, in nearly fifty years, Epifanio merely shrugged and said the risk was too great. Greater than certain starvation?

Why was Alonso pulling his sleeve?

"Name the mare, dreamer."

"*Sí*, name the mare."

What were they talking about? Who was to name what mare?

"It is the custom, Martin," Don Jaime said gently.

"*Sí*, the segundo must name his first mare."

"But, Don Jaime, I did not know I was to name

her," Martin said, blushing and casting about desperately for an appropriate name. They could not expect him to give the golden chestnut mare just any name. It must be a very special name, and at this moment he could not think of any, any at all. Everyone was silent. They were waiting for him. Why hadn't Epifanio warned him? He wished the Doña Marta was here. She would help him. She always had. The previous domador's wife was the closest thing to a mother he had ever known. She was old and ill now, but he went to see her almost every day. That was it. Of course!

"I name the mare Marta, in honor of the Doña Marta, the wife of the last domador of the Roca Estancia," Martin said, very solemnly.

"Well done. A name we can all say with pride," Don Jaime said warmly. "We all rejoice with Doña Marta in the honor you have done her and us."

"Thank you, Don Jaime." Martin bowed slightly in what he supposed was the custom. He felt silly. But perhaps Don Jaime would not be so quick to sell a horse named after the Doña Marta. Don Jaime also visited the old lady daily.

"Domador, your nephew speaks well. We will need him along with my sons when we are no longer patrón and domador, no?"

"Oh, he named the mare well enough," Epifanio admitted grudgingly, "but he has much to learn yet." Epifanio acted as if he were not pleased with the thought that anyone might take his place.

Alonso threw up his hands in mock horror. "Can he never be pleased, this ancient gaucho?" he asked.

"The day of the gaucho is over," Epifanio grunted.

"But tonight we celebrate success, your success, Martin, and yours, Epifanio. Alonso, play us a tune, my son." Don Jaime handed his eldest boy a harmonica. Even Epifanio smiled, for like all Argentines he loved the harmonica, and Alonso played very well. Everyone was quiet as Alonso put the harmonica to his lips.

> *En el alma mía*
> *Solo hay dolor*
> *Desde que te fuiste.*
>
> In my soul
> There is only sadness
> Since you went away.

The men sang softly. This was a song the conquistadores had brought from Spain three hundred years before, and they had all first heard it in their cradles. Every gaucho loved to remember that he was descended from the conquistadores. Martin knew Alonso had chosen this song for his father and for Epifanio. It had been a long day and Martin lay back on a chaise longue. The fireflies and the stars seemed to fuse over the pampa now. His moment was over, and in spite of his resolves, Martin fell asleep.

He woke hearing angry voices.

"If the drought continues, and it will, we will lose half the herd. That's a fact," Martin heard Epifanio shout.

"If not more."

"And the sheep? What about the sheep? Not so many?" Don Jaime asked sadly.

"Yes, so many. We have better than two thousand sheep this year. And if the drought continues one

more month, we will be lost. Better to send them all
to slaughter now than try to make it through and
fail." Epifanio stood before Don Jaime, shaking his
finger at the patrón who was four times his size.

"My whole flock? But they are thoroughbreds.
We wouldn't get a peso a pound, Domador." Don
Jaime used the formal term when he disapproved.

"Better a peso a pound while they are still fat than
the same or less for a bag of bones."

"Well, maybe it will rain," Alonso said, trying to
make peace. He knew more about polo than ranching, Martin thought. He sat straight up.

"I tell you it will not rain," Epifanio said gloomily.
He was called "the weathervane" because he could
forecast rain with more certainty than anyone else
in the north of Argentina. Men came every day to
ask him if it would rain.

"It is early yet and it may! And if it does not? Then
will be the time to slaughter my sheep. No?" Don
Jaime poured himself more vermouth.

"*Sí*, Don Jaime."

"No, Don Jaime," Epifanio insisted. "If we
slaughter the sheep now, we at least gain fodder for
the horses. Later, neither will gain, and the sheep will
be dehydrated."

"Doña Marta said there is pasture in Calamuchita.
Why can't we drive the horses south to where it does
rain?" Alonso had asked the question burning on
Martin's tongue.

"If Doña Marta were not so old, she would no longer dream," Don Jaime replied, angry now. "The drive would kill them in their weakened condition. There is only one water hole in three days ride."

"Besides, the two mountain ranges are impassable now," Epifanio added.

"But they've been crossed."

"Not by a full herd in a dozen years," Don Jaime sighed. "Alonso, Epifanio and I were boys when Doña Marta's husband drove our herd last to Calamuchita. My brother Miguel was patrón then, and he left the ranch to care for itself as best it could and went too. They saved only half the horses. With his soul he saved those horses and at great cost to the ranch at home. And when the hail hit them the next year, it hit Miguel also, and he died that winter of a broken heart. Whatever will be, will be. It is the way of the world."

"*Sí*, it is fate." The men shook their heads slowly.

"It is not fate; it is pure accident and it is poisoning —everyone's judgment," Alonso replied pleadingly.

"It is said there is green grass up to their manes in Calamuchita. Wouldn't it be worth trying just once again?" Martin stood up, excited and hopeful. This *must* be the way to save the Arabians!

"No. Too risky. We do better to make what we can from the sheep now," Epifanio replied shortly.

"But even if we slaughter the sheep now, we have fodder for little more than a month. What then? Do

we sit like Don Sanchez our neighbor, listening while
his horses cry all night in hunger?" Martin asked, too
determined to push the drive to realize he was con-
tradicting his uncle in public.

"*We*, Martin? Does riding segundo for one horse
give you the deciding voice on the ranch today?
Basta!" His voice was withering.

"But the boy is right about the fodder. How long
would it last?" Don Jaime asked.

"Longer for two hundred and fifty horses than
two thousand sheep. You have no choice, Jaime."
Epifanio said this last gently. He used the patrón's
name only once in a great while.

"No, no! I can not slaughter all the sheep now.
I cannot! That is final!" Don Jaime drew himself to
full height. He was the owner. The sheep would stay.

"Then lose your herd. The finest Arabians in Argentina! Ha! They'll be no good for plowhorses in
three months!" Epifanio bellowed. He stalked off the
veranda and down the driveway into the night.

"Are you God, that you know it will not rain?"
Don Jaime yelled after him, shaking his fist.

"E-pi-fan-i-o Gui-men-ez," echoed a voice from
across the pampa, a proud defiant call that cut the
silence of the hot, still night.

"You think you are an eagle, but you are only a
chicken hawk, Epifanio Guimenez!" Don Jaime
yelled back. There were only hoofbeats in reply.

"Well, go on to bed, boys. There is work to be

done tomorrow. Still work, thank God." Don Jaime
shooed them off the veranda. They could hear him
pacing back and forth alone as they left.

"What a time for them to fight, eh?" Alonso asked.

"My uncle would never have left like that if he
were not angry with me."

"But you were right about the pasture."

"So? I should not have contradicted him. He is my
uncle and my domador. But, Alonso, he'll get over it
—and I've got an idea. Can you and Carlos go with me
to Doña Marta's tomorrow?"

"Of course; there is still room for hope."

"*Hasta mañana*, then?"

"*Hasta mañana*."

Martin thought carefully as he walked back across
the dry, crackling fields to the adobe house he shared
with his uncle. Epifanio was not home yet but this
was not surprising. The old gaucho often rode the
pampa all night if he was upset or had a problem.
Epifanio said that by realizing how insignificant he
was before the stars and the land, his problem also
became small and easily solved. One could only hope
that it would be so.

Martin rolled his sheepskin, which served for both
mattress and blanket, to the front of the house where
there was a light breeze, and before he had time to
find Orion in the summer sky, he was asleep.

The next afternoon Martin and Carlos and Alonso
rode toward the *casita* of Doña Marta. They carried

a certificate bearing the name of the mare, Marta.

Doña Marta lived a mile or so from the main estancia in a shady hollow of weeping willow trees. Here she raised chickens and rabbits and supplied eggs for the entire estancia. Her adobe house had three small rooms and was whitewashed. When Martin was a little boy he had thought it a mansion. Perhaps this was because Doña Marta's house had windows and curtains and a sofa like the estancia of Don Jaime. Then he had hoped Epifanio would marry Doña Marta's fat daughter so they could live in her house. It had been several years since he had wished this, and now he had almost forgotten it.

Doña Marta was always in bed now, not so much because she was sick as because she was very old. She laughed and said people were mistaken in thinking her wise just because she was no longer beautiful but wrinkled. Yet it was certainly true that whenever anyone on the ranch had a problem, he came to visit the Doña Marta and left refreshed. Don Jaime himself came every day.

The three boys were bringing her a problem this afternoon. They were pleased that there were no other horses tied to the hitching post. They would have her to themselves. They trotted their horses peacefully through the gate and down into the hollow filled with ancient weeping willows. The stillness there quieted even Carlos, who had been complaining because he had not been invited to the celebration for

Martin the night before.

For some botanical reason the weeping willows grew only in this one hollow on all the ranch. There were no others within twenty miles. Some said Doña Marta had planted them herself when she came to the ranch as a bride, some seventy years before, but no one knew for sure. She only smiled mysteriously if anyone asked. For many years now they had provided a cool summer magic for people and a sanctuary for parrots.

Hundreds of parrots wheeled chattering high into the air as the boys came close, only to settle again in a few moments.

"She knows we're here now," Carlos said. He was as plump and blond and red-cheeked as Martin was tall and skinny and tanned almost black. They were different also in that Martin wanted to be a domador and go to school as little as possible, while Carlos wanted to be a lawyer and work on the ranch as little as possible. He was the patrón's youngest son, and he and Martin had been constant companions since they were babies.

Now they tethered their horses and went to the open door where Juana, Doña Marta's fat daughter, waited.

"Ah, Doña Marta has suitors today," she said, teasing.

"Epifanio sends his regrets, but he has a ranch to run," Carlos replied wickedly. It was well known that

Juana had sighed in vain over Martin's uncle for thirty years.

"I hear he and Don Jaime had words last night?"

"Now *how* could you ever hear such a thing," Carlos said archly.

"How is Doña Marta?" Martin asked quickly. He did not want to discuss the fight. His uncle was not speaking to *anyone* today.

"And I also hear that Martin went to a celebration last night, but that the children of the ranch were not invited."

Carlos flushed. He did not understand why his father had excluded him from Martin's party.

"My father feels that one must prove he is an adult before he attends the councils," Alonso said with an arch glance at his little brother. It was well known that Don Jaime considered Carlos lazy because he preferred reading books to riding the range.

"And what have you done?" Carlos asked hotly.

"Perhaps he has only grown tall, and that is just a matter of time," Juana said soothingly. She had pricked Carlos and had no wish to punish him further. "The Doña Marta is as well as we have any right to hope," she added to Martin as she ushered them into the cool room where the tiny white-haired lady lay propped up on pillows. Juana knew the last thing the boys wanted was a detailed medical report. She would have the opportunity for that when the older women of the ranch came. They often saved themselves the

trouble and expense of a doctor by copying Doña
Marta's prescriptions.

Doña Marta grinned happily as they perched on
the edge of her bed. It was a toothless grin, since she
never bothered with dentures unless Don Jaime was
visiting. He had given them to her and might be
offended if she neglected his gift. But his sons would
not tell on her.

"Segundo! Come sit here on the bed," she ordered.

"Segundo? How did you know so soon?"

"Amigo, it is the great news of the estancia today.
Even the chickens speak of your speed and grace.
You do well, Martin. Today a segundo but tomorrow
a domador!"

She kissed him on both cheeks, giving her words
the effect of prophecy. Martin blushed a deep red.
Suddenly he stood up and said, "But Epifanio says I
have much to learn yet."

No one was more surprised than Martin by his
words. The Doña Marta watched him quietly for a
few moments before answering.

"And he will teach you everything, my son," she
said. Then she laughed and went on lightly. "And
who will teach me? Carlos, will you teach me the
law? Or perhaps the patroncito will show me how to
play the harmonica?"

"But you would need to wear your teeth to play
the harmonica," Alonso reminded the old lady.

"Then I will listen to you, instead," she answered,

laughing.

Martin wanted to thank Doña for reminding him that Epifanio was his teacher, but somehow he could not. Instead, he handed her the certificate showing the mare's genealogy and her name as Marta. "Don Jaime asked that I bring you this."

She reached for her glasses from the table beside her bed and, putting them on, carefully read the document through twice. A tear rolled down her cheek. She brushed it away quickly.

"I hope she is beautiful," she said.

"Not so beautiful as you, señora, but Martin thought he caught a certain resemblance," Carlos answered.

"Just make sure her training is a credit to me. I can't have people saying I'm a devil at my age." Doña Marta winked. She kept hold of Martin's hand and patted it absently as if there were something more she wished to say. "You must be a credit to both domadors, Martin. Since the day Epifanio pulled you from the burning automobile that killed your mother and father and brought you to me in his poor charred arms, you have been my son, too. But don't let me turn into a sentimental old lady—tell me why you are *really* here today!"

Martin could say nothing. Doña Marta had never spoken of the accident before.

"To honor you," Carlos said quickly.

"Nonsense."

"We came to ask you to convince my father and Epifanio to let us drive the horses south to Calamuchita where there is water," Alonso began.

"We cannot expect rain for three months, my uncle says. He also says we will lose half the herd even if we sell the sheep at market this month," Martin went on quietly.

"Didn't your husband, the old domador, drive them south across the mountains to Calamuchita?" Carlos asked innocently. She had often told them of the drive.

"He nearly died of heat, starvation, and thirst on the way, Carlos. And this year it is said that the mountain lions, the pumas, are very bad. The first pass has been closed by falling rocks. But if you should get through? The mountains beyond are wild and dry, except for freak storms that sweep through the canyons like tornadoes. Do you know what you are doing?"

"No, but we are willing to learn," Martin replied.

"What does your uncle say, Martin, and your father, Alonso?" Doña Marta spread her arms out on the white bed. She closed her eyes and lay back among the pillows. The boys waited quietly until she opened them again.

"Uncle Epifanio says to kill the sheep and give the pasture to the horses."

"And my father says he won't. He says Epifanio is a chicken hawk."

"And both say a drive is tempting the fates."

"We must leave fate to God who understands it. And so they are locking horns again," she said, as if the fight were a great joke. "It is kind of them to entertain the gauchos."

"Have you thought about whether you would take the whole herd or only the stallions?" she went on idly.

"I think we must take them all. We must take the colts and the mares if we want a strong herd next year and the year after."

"It will make your trip ten times harder, Martin. But you are right. Jaime will not like me for interfering, but it is for his own good. I cannot promise a thing. But go out, all of you, and scout the mountains for passes clear enough to accommodate two hundred and fifty horses. Look for water holes and for fodder. Remember that horses can eat moss from the rocks if there is nothing else. Go tomorrow if possible. There is no time to lose." Doña Marta sat straight up now, frail to a transparency but sparkling with the new adventure.

Juana signaled that they were tiring her, and they started to leave.

"Ah, Juana, they do not tire me. Old ladies tire me. These boys are like the thunderstorms that lend me their energy. All right, all right, go now then. But bring me a map when you come again—a map that covers the terrain from here to Calamuchita, a map with elevations. And, one more thing, study the geography. You must know every group of trees and every possible stream as if you had lived along the whole route all your life. Who knows? Perhaps an old lady and three boys may save a herd." She closed her eyes, still smiling.

"Your uncle and your father would skin you alive if they knew what you were up to, and they should be told," Juana whispered as they left the room.

"Remember, this is our secret. Not a word to anyone. Don Jaime and I will discuss the weather when he visits tonight," Doña Marta added.

The boys grinned at Juana. They knew she would never tell anything that her mother wanted kept a secret.

"Take care of my horse, Martin."

"She will be a credit to you, Doña Marta."

"With God's help you will all be a credit to me. *Hasta la vista, amigos.*"

"*Hasta la vista, señora.*"

Epifanio's Decision

A WEEK PASSED. SEVEN DAYS. THEY WERE SWELTER-
ing days when sheep and horses foraged dying grass
down to the roots and sprawled restlessly in the hot
dirt. Dust rose in suffocating clouds wherever Martin
walked, subsiding only to surge again if a dog chased
a rabbit or a chicken scurried for a relatively cool
spot under a bush to wait for the night. Everyone
waited for the night, but when it finally came the air
was not much cooler. On Thursday clouds gathered
and hope spread like wildfire through the ranch, but
by sundown the sky was as crimson as ever and the
clouds had vanished without leaving a trace. Neither
Epifanio nor the horses had been fooled for a minute.
They had looked at the clouds and continued work-

46

ing and foraging. To all the gauchos who rode to ask Epifanio if the clouds meant rain, he only shook his head and shook it still harder when they argued with him. He and Don Jaime still did not speak, but as Doña Marta said, there was little pleasant to say anyhow.

Martin and Carlos drove their horses farther and farther to find pasture. Now they pastured high in rocky mountains where a sudden mesa provided only brief respite for two hundred and fifty horses. The pasture on Don Sanchez' side of the mesa was already gone because he had used it for three weeks. His horses whinnied almost constantly and burrowed in the dirt, hunting for a forgotten root. Don Sanchez, a proud old Spaniard whose family had come to Argentina with the conquistadores, sat astride his horse on the edge of the pasture almost every day, and his face showed a terrible pain as he heard his horses cry out. He would curse the vultures and throw stones, which fell far short of reaching them, as they circled endlessly overhead.

The Roca Estancia horses were not in much better shape, Martin thought, as he watched them plodding about until they found grass and then eating greedily as if they might never find more. They were always sniffing these days, and the dry creeks and drying mud holes tortured their cracked nostrils. They would roll in the mud and whinny piteously when the caking, drying dirt pulled their hides. Their coats were no longer sleek, but shaggy and filthy. Martin felt each evening that he could not stand it any more. Then each morning he rode out again with the horses, and by noon was thinking of his uncle's description of horses' bones whitening in heaps across the pampa during the last drought.

He felt worst of all about the golden chestnut mare he had helped to break and named after Doña Marta. The mare was saddle broken now, and he rode her every day. She was an intelligent and spirited but obedient horse, and she already knew three gaits. Don Jaime would ordinarily keep such a beauty, but under the circumstances he planned to sell her at the next stock auction, where he would get next to nothing for her because no one else had water either. Doña Marta would rather see her namesake sold than see her die of thirst, Epifanio had said roughly.

"If she dies of thirst, what does it matter who watches?" Martin had replied.

"It matters. Ask Don Sanchez," Epifanio had said grimly.

Martin would have gone crazy if he had not been working on a solution, if he and Alonso and Carlos and Doña Marta had not been planning the drive that would take their horses out of this dust bowl and south to Calamuchita, where they would have green grass up to their manes. It would have been better if Doña Marta had not been so sure they must keep the plan a secret. Martin did not like keeping secrets from

Epifanio. But she said they must have all the facts before they bothered Don Jaime and Epifanio. They must know their route: the terrain, where there was water and fodder, and where they might find passes through the treacherous mountains. She found books on geography and history and sent the boys out to scout the land they must cover.

They found a pass through the Pocho Mountains the first evening, as they rode toward Pocho. It was filled with rock and debris and needed clearing before two hundred and fifty horses could hope to pass.

Martin and Carlos had to be on the ranch every day to herd the Arabians, but Alonso had no specific duties since he had just returned from six years at the university. So he was elected to clear the seven-mile pass. He told his father he would be away a few days, called himself Hercules, and hired three men from Pocho with a truck. They worked for five days from the first light until the last flicker of the sunset; and when they were through, the pass was clear. During this time Alonso also found one good water hole and a patch of dry but edible pampa grass.

"The men I had working thought it unusual that I worked so hard for the government. I could not tell them our plans, but I hope they were not right. If we do not take the horses, I have made the people of Pocho a present of my labor and all the money I was saving to buy a guitar," Alonso commented wryly when he returned, sunburned and aching.

"It is good for you. You look strong and handsome tonight. But tell me if you found a pass through the Sierras Grandes, the big mountains?" Doña Marta asked, patting Alonso's calloused hand.

"We can reach the Pampa Achala—here—and cross it easily if we wait for the wind to die down. But I did not have time to go farther, and I do not know what lies beyond. I did not dare sleep out by myself because all the people speak of nothing but the pumas, the mountain lions. They are hungry too, it seems, and I am so tender. I would not mind, except that my father needs me to inherit these horses we are saving. No?"

"Why begrudge the poor puma his dinner? Carlos can inherit the horses," Martin teased.

"No, Alonso is right. We need him for the drive. Besides, I want to be a lawyer, not a rancher; and you know my father would never let me escape if there was no one else to inherit the horses," Carlos moaned.

"And have you been using that legal mind on the books I lent you?" Doña Marta asked.

"*Sí, señora.*"

Since Carlos and Martin had to be in the fields during the day, their job had been to learn the geography and everything else they could about the area they were to cross. Doña Marta quizzed them on what they had learned every night, mile by mile. For by this time they had decided that the only plausible route was through the Pocho Mountains and on across the long pampa between them and the Great Sierra Mountains. These they would have to cross at the Pampa Achala, the highest pampa in all Argentina. They had to cross here because this was the one spot that had water, food, and a large enough level spot to rest and relax their horses. Only Alonso and the Doña Marta had ever seen this plain, though every boy in Argentina dreamed of the battles fought there and the famous men who had crossed it. None of the four had seen the land the horses must travel the last three or four days of the drive, the land beyond the pampa.

"Therefore," said Doña Marta, "you must know this land even better. What is the climate, what is the foliage, and what snakes and animals lie in wait for you? The horses will be very tired by this time, and you will have to think for them. You should even know how many trees are in this Bosque Alegre—"

"And how many board feet they will provide if chopped down?" Carlos asked. "Well, that shouldn't be hard. It looks like just a little clump on the map. I'll check the encyclopedia."

"Well, it's the only clump, so I hope it means water," Martin added, studying the map. "But, Doña Marta, we don't even know if we're really going until we talk to Don Jaime and my uncle. They both think the drive is going against nature after—"

"After the hailstorm? Every rancher has a hailstorm or a plague that stops his adventuring spirit until one day—" Doña Marta spread her hands expressively.

"It would take more dynamite than I used on the pass to change *my* father. Ever since I can remember, every single up-to-date improvement on the ranch has been stymied by that hailstorm."

"Just like Epifanio and the doma. Everything must be done the way the conquistadores did it. If the conquistadores had stuck to tradition, they'd never have come to Argentina in the first place," Martin added intensely.

"To live well today, one must know of those who have gone before so one does not repeat their mistakes. And to be a domador, Segundo, you must know the exact moment to act. When we are ready, perhaps Don Jaime, too, will be ready to try an old route once more," she said quietly, closing her eyes. "Patience," she whispered as they left the room.

"Patience! She can have patience because she's not watching those horses dry up!" Martin exploded to Carlos the next night as they were studying the map on the ground before the *casita* Martin and Epifanio shared. The little adobe house sat on a rise and caught any breeze. But tonight there was none, and the boys had eaten dry galletas rather than build a fire to barbecue the steaks they usually had for dinner. So they were still hungry, hot, discouraged, and tired. The sun was an orange ball just sinking beyond the pampa below them.

"Or little boys playing cowboys. Maybe she is just keeping us busy and out of trouble. How many weeks since you've heard anyone laugh, Martin?"

"And how many days since you two have done anything but ruin your good eyes over those maps?" asked Epifanio, coming up behind them. How long had he been there? What had he heard?

"Even *if* Don Jaime decided to risk a drive—and you do not even begin to realize the risks, little heroes —what makes you think he would ask you two to plan the route? For how many years have you planned horse drives that you feel competent to decide the route for one of the finest herds in Argentina?" Epifanio sounded pettish and exhausted, but he also made good sense. Both boys hung their heads and said nothing.

"First you know we should make a drive, and then you know how we should travel. The universe begins and ends in your wisdom?"

"We never said we were wise or knew the best routes, but no one else does anything. Nothing. And I don't want to see Marta just a heap of bones whitening in the sun after the vultures are through with her," Martin blurted out furiously.

"Martin, be quiet! Careful, *amigo!*" Carlos said this sharply, horrified that Martin should yell at his uncle, and afraid he might reveal the extent of their planning.

"It is just so hot," Martin mumbled by way of apology.

"Marta, eh? Well, may I look at this worn out map of yours?" Epifanio asked casually, taking the map and tracing the route with his forefinger. He traced it over several times and sat looking out at the prairie for a long while in silence. He sat on both heels, and in his black bombachas, white shirt, and black gaucho hat he looked like the cowboy on the picture post-cards.

"The same route. But the pass through the Pochos is blocked—or was a month ago." he said, puzzled.

Oho, so he had checked into it.

"Alonso had it cleared this week. He used his guitar money," both boys said at once. This was the first time Epifanio had admitted to any interest, and yet he had ridden over to check the pass.

Epifanio raised an eyebrow and waited for the boys to say more.

"We thought we could cross the pampa by night when it is relatively cool and reach Pocho in two or three days. We could get water at Pocho—"

"Where?"

"Here. Alonso found a water hole."

"The patroncito has learned more than polo this last week. Well, and then where will we go?"

"We?"

"Then comes the problem," Carlos continued. "None of us has ever been beyond the Pampa Achala. We don't have any idea what we'd find beyond that, and it is too far to scout and get back before—"

"You did not ask *me*," Epifanio said.

"Have you been there?" Carlos asked.

"*I* knew you'd been there, but you weren't speaking to me."

"I always speak if there is something worth saying, Martin. But if we ever get those Arabians to the Pampa Achala and the grass is like it was when I knew the plain, we will never pull them off, not even one by one. They will think they are in heaven and settle down forever. It would almost be worth the drive just to see it again, the high pampa, and feel the low thin wind that makes a man know he's got a soul. The grass isn't so tall as it is down in the south. But there is something about it; the horses fancy it more than anything else in the world. Oh, take my—"

"Epifanio! Epifanio! Come quickly. I can't hold on!"

"Alonso!"

What was the matter? He'd gone to check the horses. What could have happened?

"Epifanio, come here and see the skunk, the snake in the grass!"

"*Caramba!* Must you wake the dead when you cannot even decide what is a snake and what a skunk? I'm coming."

All three started up the hill toward Alonso's voice at a dead run. They stumbled over rocks and bushes in the twilight.

"Here! Over here! I've had the devil's own time

bringing this thief down. You just try leading a man
roped to a horse down this sliding pile of rocks from
the high pasture!" Alonso and the man trussed up on
horseback were only shadows.

"What did he steal?" Carlos asked.

"Who is he?" Epifanio asked.

"I said I would come without being roped like a
calf," said a voice from the horse.

"I caught him with the wire cutters still in his
hand. He had just finished cutting our fences, and he
tells me he is a man of honor." Alonso's voice rang
with scorn. "Thanks to him the bony nags from next
door are eating our pasture to the roots."

"Have you watched your herd starve, day after
day, under a sky that gives nothing, not even hope?"

Even Alonso was silenced by the agony in the

man's voice. Martin and Carlos gasped. They knew
that voice. Epifanio ran to the man and cut his ropes.

"Forgive him, Don Sanchez!" Epifanio said hum-
bly. "It is Alonso, Don Jaime's oldest son, who has

been away at school the last six years. It is nearly dark and his memory is very poor, so he did not recognize you. Besides, he is an idiot!" Epifanio turned to Alonso and said this last with fury.

"He could not expect me thus."

"How long could you stand it?" Epifanio moaned.

"Don Sanchez, old friend of my father. Please forgive me, I did not know. I did not know!" Alonso took both of the old man's hands and began chafing them where he felt rope marks.

"Alonso—*chico*—do not grieve. I am proud that you would not know me for a thief. I do not know myself. I used to say you would grow up a thief when you took one apple from my tree—remember, my son? How could you possibly know that I would be the thief? I am proud that you did not know me." He staggered against his horse but pushed away all help. "What right had I to better treatment than any other thief?"

"Don't use that word! You were only saving your horses, as any honorable gaucho would," Epifanio said angrily, tears running down his cheeks. Martin had never seen his uncle cry before. He suddenly felt close to him, and wanted to put his hand in Epifanio's as he used to when he was a small boy. "And in the end, they will probably *all* die of thirst, anyway," his uncle said, bitterly.

"As mine did in the last drought. You were only a child, younger than these boys, then, eh, Epifanio?

But even you must remember the smell—the putrid smell of death creeping over a herd while most of them are still living. It drives the rest crazy, and so you lose them all. I was afraid to smell it again, and when the vultures started circling lower and lower, I knew it could not be long. I lost five hundred Arabians fifty years ago in the drought, but I was a young man and I started over. I felt I could not start over again," Don Sanchez said gently. Martin felt he had never heard such sadness in a voice before. Everyone was quiet after he spoke.

Martin could not understand why Epifanio did not say something to comfort the old man. He did not blame Don Sanchez for cutting the fence. What was there to say? They were a grain of sand in the life of the pampa? Maybe they should put the horses back in their own pasture and repair the fence. The moon was rising now and they would have light. If they let it go until morning the horses would be all mixed up, and it would take a week to get them all untangled. Martin felt very tired.

Don Sanchez spoke. "Epifanio, please pardon me. I listened to my horses cry day and night. Finally I heard nothing else. Honor came to seem emptier than the stomach of one horse. I was wrong! Send a boy for some of my men and we will rebuild tonight—now! I still know what is right!" The old man suddenly seemed to regain his energy. He stood straight up. He was a tall thin man with long white hair and a well-trimmed white goatee. He wore the traditional black bombachas and white shirt, but he also wore the black jacket and tie of a gentleman. His eyes were stern.

"There are five of us," Epifanio replied. "We do not need to disturb the whole ranch to repair this little accident."

How clever! That way no one would ever need to know. Don Sanchez' reputation would stay intact. Don Sanchez was an old gaucho, and old gauchos stood together. Martin was proud of his uncle.

"Of course, it was just a little break. A common accident. I'll go for more wire," Alonso said eagerly.

"He is strong if not bright," Epifanio said lightly. "Do you know he cleared a seven-mile mountain pass this week? Ah, you did not realize that I know everything, Alonso? Well, now you know. And after you get the wire, please leave word at the Doña Marta's that we will join them later. Your father will be there tonight. It is about another matter," he assured Don Sanchez.

"*Gracias.*" Don Sanchez bowed with dignity.

It was almost ten o'clock when Epifanio, Alonso, Carlos, and Martin guided their exhausted mounts down the steep rocky path from the high pasture. Don Sanchez had ridden toward his ranch. Somehow the act of cutting the fence and being ashamed had given him new courage. He said he would hunt new pasture in the morning, and would sell most of the herd. They had repaired the fence and driven the Sanchez horses back to their side of the mesa. Martin had hated dragging the starving horses away from the only grass they'd had in a week. And that already eaten to the ground.

Alonso had gotten a nasty nip in the arm from one gaunt and ribby mare who was not going to see her colt starve without a fight. "It is their horses or our horses, theirs or ours," Martin had repeated over and over to himself as he yanked and pulled the Sanchez horses away. He could understand why Don Sanchez cut that fence. And how long would it be before he was chopping down trees to fodder their own horses? "Our horses next," he thought. "Unless, unless, unless there is a move."

"That does it!" Epifanio called as they halted at the foot of the mountain.

"Does us in," Alonso added, applying Merthiolate to his arm.

"Well, it assures me that a lawyer leads a fine clean life. At least clean," Carlos said, looking around at his dust-coated companions. "I can't even tell who is who, except that Martin is a foot taller than Epifanio and I and only half as wide as Alonso."

They did look like black scarecrows in the moonlight, Martin thought. Behind them the mountain rose straight and barren as mountains do in Argentina. And before them the pampa twinkled with fireflies. They themselves were insignificant, nothing but talk.

"*Arriba, hombres!* We ride to the house of the Doña Marta. She desires to be the dove of peace fluttering between your father and I." Epifanio laughed.

"What's put you in such a gay mood, Epifanio? Have you been amusing yourself?"

"Your father awaits you, Patroncito. No need to clean up or explain. Doña Marta has seen many dirty gauchos who have had an *accident* to repair. *Vamos!*" Epifanio yelled. The boys stood staring at him.

"I'm going home to bed," Carlos said.

"What a splendid idea!" Alonso agreed.

"How long will that pasture last our horses?" Martin cried. He had to ask the question torturing them all.

"Martin, we will talk tomorrow when we are not tired. Tonight a beautiful lady has invited us to maté and we go!" This was a command, and three tired boys remounted their horses.

"Let's get it over with, then," Martin said without grace. They rode in silence across the field and down into the little valley of weeping willow trees. Each felt a thousand questions, but welcomed the silence and the gradual feeling of peace seeping into him and did not speak. Too much had happened today. There was a little breeze. Better to be quiet and let it cool the body a moment.

Juana did not meet them at the door. Instead they knocked and went on into the clean white room where Doña Marta lay in her enormous white bed on a heap of pillows. The old lady wore her teeth and sparkling diamond earrings tonight. She winked as they entered, and went back to the map she and Don Jaime were studying.

"Ah, working gauchos," she said finally, after Don Jaime had acknowledged their presence. "Go and wash, boys, so that I may see your faces. Yours is better covered with dust, Epifanio. Stay."

When they returned, Don Jaime and Epifanio were chatting as if they had never had a disagreement in the world. How did she manage it?

"And so you got them back on their own side of the fence. Good. We must put off starvation while we can," Don Jaime said.

Epifanio shrugged. Martin felt like shaking him.

"Would you believe that such a beautiful lady could be such a stubborn mule?" Don Jaime went on, clucking his tongue and waving his finger under Doña Marta's nose. "She is still studying maps."

"The boys have an identical map," Epifanio said, tracing the route with his finger. "I knew the way was familiar. This is the same route the old domador took, isn't it?"

"I did not tell the boys what trails to choose, but they found the same ones. Perhaps there is only one safe route to Calamuchita for two hundred and fifty horses. My husband brought the other herd in safely. Yes, and even after that famous hail you had horses enough to found this herd and the herd of Don Sanchez and of how many other neighbors. Now tell me it wasn't worthwhile!"

"Oh, I know all that. But the ranch and my brother paid the price!"

"The price for the drought, not for acting to save enough husks to seed again," she said more gently.

"Safely, she says, safely. Half lost last time, and this is the worst year for pumas in God only knows how long. The pass that Alonso cleared with his guitar money—how do you think it was covered with boulders? They fell during a flash flood that killed four men and a dozen cows in two minutes. That's how! Have you boys ever been in a stampede? Or fought angry men who did not like two hundred and fifty horses trampling their land. And suppose there is an epidemic and half the horses take sick midway between water holes? And what will you do for feed? You can't carry fodder for them. It would slow you down more than it would be worth. Besides, there is none. And there'd be no turning back—my sheep enter the pasture the minute the herd leaves, before Sanchez' nags start jumping the fence. The horses haven't even shoes, most of them," Don Jaime finished, looking directly at Epifanio.

"Or immunizations," Epifanio added.

"When will you get them?"

"Tomorrow, if the veterinarian can do it," Epifanio replied, grinning.

"Then we're going?" Martin couldn't restrain him-

self. But a look from Doña Marta quieted him. Carlos
grabbed his arm. Alonso crossed his fingers and held
them up for Martin and Carlos to see.

"You do think this whole idea is tempting the fates,
don't you, old friend?"

"Doña Marta says the herd is based on your
brother's chance."

"And you know that these conspirators have decided we should send the whole herd, the mares and
colts as well as the stallions?"

"To keep the herd it is necessary."

"Epifanio, we have known each other a long
while."

"All our lives if memory serves, Patrón."

"When will you leave?" Don Jaime spread his
hands in resignation. It was decided, but the boys
could not say a word yet. They had to sit very still.
Martin thought he would burst, but he knew that
these final decisions must be made by the men of the
ranch and only the men of the ranch.

"The day after tomorrow if we can get the inocu-
lations and the medicine for the horses. Doña Sulenita
will see to the provisions?"

"With our sons two of the conspirators? My wife
will weep for four hours and then prepare twice as
much food as you can possibly take," Don Jaime said.
"And how many men will you need?"

"Only enough to box the herd. I will take these
three useless ones and go myself to see that they keep

out of trouble."

"I am to trust my herd to three boys and an old man? And send both my sons? Why not Doña Marta here?"

"I would take her if she could ride. We cannot turn back, Don Jaime, because your sheep will have the pasture. So I want only those who do not yet know the impossible."

"Oh, I would go, I would go if I could," Doña Marta said excitedly.

"They also do not know the terrain," Don Jaime replied.

Doña Marta brought out her books and quizzed Martin and the patrón's sons. This was the time to show what she had taught them. When they were through, Don Jaime stood up and strode about the room. The tiny room shook as the enormous man paced back and forth. He was still a lusty man, muscular and tanned, and now his bright blue eyes twinkled. Finally he threw back his head and laughed. Epifanio, too, laughed. They laughed until they shook, and the rest of them watched the two gauchos in amazement.

"Yes, the time comes when the young know best," Epifanio said finally.

"My own sons. I am proud. By God, I am going to go with you! I'll do it!" Don Jaime thundered.

Epifanio shook his head sadly.

"But I will. I want to! You need me. I've been over

the whole business—Epifanio, the day of the gaucho is not over. We will ride together once more."

"Jaime, the drought remains here. Your brother went with my husband. He saved his horses with his soul, but you cared for the ranch."

Don Jaime made a face that showed he understood. "And I must again. How strange fate is, old friend! But I will ride down and meet you in Calamuchita. Agreed?"

"Agreed."

Now the boys could speak. They yelled. They pounded each other on the back. Everyone asked questions and no one answered because each was also asking another question. They all shook hands.

Doña Marta lay back on her pillows, enjoying it all. But finally she said, "There will be no more sense from any of you *locos* tonight. I am an old lady and need my beauty sleep. You are young and ugly, but you have much to do."

They took the hint and bid her good night. The wind blew gently, barely moving the weeping willow trees as the five mounted their horses. The three boys and the two gauchos rode silently back to the ranch, each deep in his own thoughts.

"Even so, we are but a grain of sand in the life of the pampa," Epifanio said to Martin as they rolled their sheepskins out under the stars. Martin nodded.

No Turning Back

THE DRY CRACKLING OF THE PAMPA GRASS SOUNDED like hundreds of firecrackers celebrating their departure. Martin had to keep reminding himself that the crackling was ominous, that it meant parched earth, and was in fact the reason they were leaving. But it sounded so gay; he felt like laughing aloud. They were on their way at last! Was it only two days ago that Epifanio and Don Jaime had finally decided they might drive the herd south to Calamuchita? So much had happened it seemed like two years. Martin listened to the thunder of hoofs, saw the struggling, straining horses under the light of the full moon, and choked on the whirling cloud of dust; and he laughed loud into the night. They were on their way!

68

The spurs on their boots and the bells on the lead mares tinkled lightly as they rode. A slight breeze broke the oppressive heat, and the moon cast a cool light over the pampa, making the endless, flat plain serene. Two hundred and fifty horses and four men were fleeing the parched earth under cover of the bright night, disturbing that serenity. Marta and the rest of the herd would have a chance to be great horses, after all. They would remain the greatest herd in all Argentina if they came through safely. And if it cost his own life, he would bring them through. He had promised Marta, whispering in her ear.

Epifanio hadn't wanted him to ride Marta tonight because she had never been on a drive and might be unreliable. But she was plodding along like a steady plowhorse, except for an occasional pull to the left, an odd habit she had not yet overcome. No one would guess she was only half broken and riding with a herd for the first time. No one but Epifanio, that is.

Martin could hear the other three whips snapping against the whine of the night wind, counterpoint to the hoofbeats. He felt the echoes of old hoofbeats on this same pampa. He was conscious of the sleeping viscachas and of the field mice beneath the baked earth crust, of the birds sleeping in bushes and nesting in the pampa grass, of the insects, very much awake and swarming everywhere. Above all, he felt the eyes of the night creatures. And he hoped they were friendly eyes.

Martin's eyes hurt from the strain of watching. The herd could be lost in half an hour if they did not watch all the time. They must watch the horses so that they did not stray, stampede, or hurt themselves. They must watch for holes and snakes and mountain lions, and they must watch for signs of a storm. There is a sudden storm that happens in Argentina and no place else on earth. It starts with hail the size of walnuts and then lets loose a torrent of rain for half an hour. These storms may be ten miles across, flooding one town and leaving absolute drought in the next. A storm like this could destroy a herd that did not seek cover. One had nearly destroyed the herd of Don Jaime's brother.

But the main thing was to keep the herd together and drive on, steadily on, especially this first night when they must reach the one and only water hole between Chepes and Pocho Pass before it became too hot for man or horse to sleep.

The horses were settling down finally. Martin felt a subtle change, a sense that the herd had accepted the drive and was no longer fighting the forward motion. They wouldn't stampede now. This was fortunate because he was settling down too. He was tired suddenly. Maybe the horses were tired too. There wasn't quite the pushing and whinnying and the stubborn sidestepping now. Not that they had given in, these proud Arabians. Far from it, Martin thought, looking at the arrogant set of their heads. They carried their tails high, and their manes flew under the moonlight. They looked more like wild spirits than horses. Still, they were working together. There was a steady pace. And above the noises of the night and the herd came the strains of an old melody Alonso was playing on his harmonica.

My ship in full sail sets out again tonight . . .
Who will travel with me through the happy night . . .

Martin looked around for Carlos. It would be good to talk to someone for a minute. The last two days had been so full of errands, injections, shopping, shoeing the horses, and pinching themselves to prove it was really true, that there had been no time to talk at all. Carlos was over to the left. He was having trouble keeping several frisky colts in line. Martin moved over to give him a hand. Epifanio and Alonso were riding toward the front of the herd and would not see that he was in trouble.

"Slow and easy, Marta, take it easy," he reassured the mare. "Tomorrow you may rest, and I will ride Gatito. Every gaucho has his string of horses, his tropilla. You and Gatito are my tropilla." Martin wished he *did* own the two horses. Someday—

"*Hola*, Carlos!"

"*Hola*, Martin. *Amigo*, bring me that little devil." Martin swung his boleadoras to catch a colt by one leg. The three rocks at the end of the lariat swung expertly; and when caught and freed, the little colt was glad enough to scurry back with the others, neighing piteously.

"You'd think I was killing that one," Martin grumbled.

"I missed her three times. Thank you. You know, I wasn't sure at first whether you were a mountain lion or just another night noise," Carlos said, revealing that he was not only tired but frightened.

"That is what he gets for staying indoors reading all the time," Martin thought without particular sympathy. He had always envied Carlos's school marks. The drive would be good for him.

"Carlos, the mountain lion makes no noise at all, so don't bother listening for him. The pumas won't bother us so soon, anyhow, because they like to size up a situation first. And Epifanio says that for some strange reason the puma likes the smell of a man. He will seldom attack us, but usually only colts that have strayed away from our scent."

"Maybe, but Alonso says men have been killed by pumas lots of times," Carlos replied.

"Alonso's an old woman. A puma only kills in self-defense or for food."

"Who told you? A puma? Haven't you ever heard the old saying, 'pride goes before a fall'? Better watch out, Martin, or the puma might not like your smell," Carlos said, only half teasing.

"*Amigo*, am I . . . preaching again?" Martin asked,

73

contrite. Carlos was his best friend.

"Well, not exactly. It's more as if you want to take on the world. You can't fight with everyone, Martin. What's wrong?"

"Oh, I had a fight with Epifanio again this afternoon. He was training Marta the gaucho way, and I want to train her as the Indians do, without violence. Carlos, he *promised* I could train her," Martin said gloomily. He had told his uncle he did not intend to use the quirt and whip on Marta, but would use hand control. Then he had found Epifanio training her the gaucho way, and all his uncle would say was that she would be dangerous on the drive. Couldn't he, Martin, have been the judge of that? Epifanio never let him decide anything that mattered.

"Martin, if we bring these horses through, they may be all that is left of the whole ranch. As you know, I am not interested in ranching, but even I can see that Epifanio feels responsible. Isn't it enough to save Marta?" Carlos asked, his rosy face and blond hair completely dust-covered. Only his concerned blue eyes shone through. "Oh, I am a fine one to talk. Not only am I scared like a girl but I'm sweating like a pig." He laughed.

"I know it's enough to get Marta through. He didn't want me to ride her tonight either and I shouldn't have, but she *is* trained. I know Epifanio is the leader, but I guess it's just that . . . he's also my uncle. And I yell first and think later. Not only that, but I ache in every bone in my body. No wonder—"

"I know—the day of the gaucho is over," Carlos finished. He smiled wryly.

"How do you avoid arguing with your father?" Martin asked. Privately he thought Carlos envied him the ability to say what he thought, but it would be nice to be able to keep his mouth shut once in a while.

"Perhaps we just have not begun," the boy answered gently. Carlos suddenly cut through the horses and quickly nudged a stumbling colt to her feet. She found her mother and began searching for milk. The other horses edged back into the void and regained the cadence of the drive. Carlos rejoined Martin.

"Doesn't Epifanio *ever* stop?" he asked. "He should be calling a rest stop soon, don't you think?"

Martin said nothing. He hoped so. On shorter drives they stopped every two hours or so, and they'd been riding at least four hours now. But he did not know what was practiced on a long drive and could not bring himself to admit this. He had already admitted how tired he was and that he'd fought again with Epifanio. That was enough. Martin could barely make out his uncle and Alonso through the dust cloud in which they rode. He could barely hear the crack of their whips above the sound of the hoofbeats. He could only just keep himself awake enough to stay on Marta. What a first drive she was having!

How could Carlos worry about pumas and night sounds? How could he even think? They stumbled into holes so often now that it became a part of the rhythm, and he and Marta just rolled with the extra plunge and jerk. He swatted insect bites so often, he wondered what else kept him awake. Of course, he would like to stop, yearned to stop and sleep for fourteen hours. But suddenly he knew they would not. They could not stop now until they reached the water hole. The horses were too tired. They would never get them started again.

And he was right. Not until daybreak, until that moment of morning shared by the night and the day, when the birds begin to rise and circle overhead, did he feel a slowing. By this time he and Carlos had long since given up any hope of ever stopping. They were glued to their saddles, mute from the impossible strain of moving their mud-caked face muscles, and deaf to any sound but pounding hoofbeats.

Nevertheless, they were still helping stumbling colts, retrieving stragglers, and they even felt the gradual slowing. They nodded when Alonso galloped back and said they were camping by the water hole ahead. Martin dimly remembered the water hole marked and circled in red on the big map at Doña Marta's peaceful ranchito. Were there trees? He saw only bush willows and mesquite. But maybe that would be enough cover, enough for him surely. Enough for Carlos.

"Halt, halt, halt, halt," he thought in rhythm with the cadence.

"Epifanio says we are quitting early today because we have reached the water hole. But we must ride again at five and really cover territory tonight," Alonso announced cheerfully. "Carlos, is that you?" He slapped his brother on the back. Carlos almost fell off his horse.

"I just wish this were the night we were sleeping at Condor Inn at Pampa Achala," Carlos said.

"Between sheets," added Martin.

"If the innkeeper takes us in, you mean," Alonso warned.

"He has to. It's the custom," Martin retorted.

"Sometimes customs are made to be broken. Two hundred and fifty horses are noisy guests. My father's telegram was not answered and there is no phone."

"Ha. Don't worry. They have to take us in." Martin realized wryly that he was counting on tradition now, and for weeks he'd been condemning Epifanio for the same thing.

"Well, it's all the same to me. I don't care where I sleep, but let's get to it." Carlos yawned.

"Oh, it won't be long now. Just look at the stars. I'll teach you the constellations one night if you wish," Alonso went on happily. He had apparently enjoyed the ride.

"I can't see them through the dust," Martin groaned.

"I can't even open my eyes," Carlos added.

"You two aren't much better company than Epifanio," Alonso said as he pivoted his black horse to
return.

"Pot calling the kettle black," Carlos called after
him.

Alonso whirled his horse once more. "Oh, I almost
forgot to ask if you lost any horses—as far as you
know. And don't forget that we have to slap salve
on the wounds yet."

Both boys shook their heads. No, they had not lost
any horses as far as they knew, but they had forgotten
about having to put salve on the animals. What a
horror! Before they could sleep they must find and
apply salve and peroxide to any lacerations, new or
old, on the exhausted horses. "Providing we can even
find them through this dust," Martin thought
dismally.

"You may tell Epifanio that we can not spare salve
for the horses because we need it all for my raw behind," Carlos finally groaned.

"We have enough salve for your ample behind
and the horses as well, my dear brother." Alonso
waved and galloped off again, shooting the dust into
a cyclone behind him.

"How can you have a brother like *that*," Martin
groaned.

"Two hundred and fifty backsides, one thousand
legs, five hundred sides, and two hundred and fifty

biting heads—and they all require salve. And each horse determined to have his wound left strictly alone and willing to defend his privacy with four good kicking hoofs. Don Sanchez' starving nags were nothing compared to this horror, *amigo!*" Carlos promised.

"Well, we're never going to reach that water hole anyhow. It was probably just a mirage," Martin returned. Ten minutes before, Martin could have sworn the water hole was just in front of them, but now it seemed farther away than ever. The sky was still a pale waiting color, with only a rim of pink on the horizon. Birds were whirling into the sky and singing for their breakfast. A flock of ducks had been pacing them for perhaps half an hour, breaking formation, scattering, and then returning.

"I could keep a perfect formation if all I had to do was fly, too," Carlos complained of the ducks.

"Let's fly, then. I want to fly. I want to fly!" Martin shouted to Carlos, waving his arms madly. Carlos waved back, and in a moment they were both laughing hysterically. Suddenly, they stopped, for theirs was the only sound. The hoofbeats, which had reverberated for so many hours that the hearing of them was second nature, had stopped. The herd had stopped! They were at the water hole! Their laughter dropped into embarrassment, and they looked around to see if Epifanio and Alonso had caught them.

But the tiny old gaucho and the huge young man

were kneeling by the water hole splashing water all over themselves. All around them, but keeping their distance, the horses were pushing and shoving for their share of the water. Low growing willow and mesquite fanned out from the water hole, but beyond this lay only the pampa grass. Far off to the left Martin saw two houses. They and their matchstick fences and meager shade trees seemed dwarfed by the pampa. Martin wondered if the four of them and their herd also seemed out of place here. Toward the horizon rose outcroppings of rock and the beginning of the foothills to the Pocho Mountains.

"Look at Gatito, Martin, look at him push," Carlos said, and they both looked at the young roan stallion pushing and shoving his way to the water.

"He's got more spirit than me. Good old Gatito."

"You ride him tonight, no? Well, let's get going on that salve before we can only save one side of each horse from infection," Carlos said, indicating with horror the problems of turning over a sleeping Arabian.

"Look at them. It is so pleasant to ride they do not even get down from their horses!" Epifanio greeted them as he and Alonso walked up, dripping wet.

"No wonder there are no true gauchos any more," Carlos retorted as he and Martin jumped down and gave their mounts a whack, sending them in the direction of the water hole.

"Surely this little trot did not tire *you*, Carlos?"

"It taught me a lesson. Law is the profession for me. All gauchos are by profession insane," Carlos answered, and ducked Epifanio's lariat. Epifanio swung again and caught him by the heels, trussing him like a calf.

"What did you say, little hero?"

"I said that you swing the lariat very well, yes, very well," he said, and Epifanio released him with a grin.

"Segundo, is law also the profession for you?" he asked quietly, looking into Martin's eyes.

Martin shook his head, no. "I learned why there is no turning back."

"Listen!" Epifanio said gently. "Have you ever heard the music of the pampa grass!"

The boys listened. The white spears were touched with color so that they blended like cloud surfaces in the distance. Gradually they heard what felt like a low murmur. The longer they listened, the louder and more insistent the murmur felt, moving over the pampa. It was an eerie sound in the still dawn.

"Brrr," Carlos said, and Epifanio gave him a severe look.

Finally Epifanio spoke. "It is true that one can only see the sun rise in the wilderness. Rows of houses, automobiles, lines of wash—God did not mean them to interrupt the beauty of the dawn. It is different out here, no?"

"*Sí*, it is different," Martin agreed.

"*Bueno*, Segundo. The poor horses. Give them the salve quickly and do not let them bite you for your help."

The boys and Epifanio moved through the horses quickly, automatically. The horses did not protest. Perhaps they were too tired to care, or felt the work no more than flies through the caked dust, worth no more effort or resistance than a flick of the tail. Many had fetlocks scraped from stepping into vizcacha holes. Martin rubbed raw elbows and bits and ragged ears. But most of the lacerations were below the knee. And there were no snake bites, no signs of the dreaded swelling that meant death in many cases. Martin looked over at his dust-covered friend, Carlos. He looked as if he had rolled in flour and emerged plumper and blonder than ever.

Finally it was all over. Epifanio dismantled his saddle to make his bed. Alonso was studying the map.

"We move into the foothills tonight and should reach the pass by tomorrow night, Epifanio?"

"*Sí*, we go into no-man's-land."

"No-man's-land? It didn't look that bad."

"They call it that because no one knows what he may find—or what may find him."

"What do you mean?" Carlos asked.

"That you must watch out for pumas and snakes and—just keep alert the next two days. But we'll discuss it later. If you are not asleep within the hour, it will be too hot to get to sleep. There is asado if you want food. *Buenas noches*," he said and rolled over with his back to them. He was snoring before they straightened up.

"He's a cheerful soul," Alonso said as they all stood looking down at Epifanio.

"How can he go to sleep after a statement like that? I know I can't," Carlos added.

"Don't worry. I told Epifanio I would take the first watch and he's just trying to help me stay awake," Alonso said, laughing uneasily.

"You two grown-ups decide things between you, don't you?" Martin said moodily. Epifanio and Alonso seemed to think he and Carlos were still children. However, he was too tired to fight; and when Alonso shrugged, Martin went to the saddlebags and pulled out three small loaves of *galleta*. He held one out to each of his friends.

"Thank God. I would have died of starvation before I'd have built a fire," Carlos said.

The three boys sat on their sheepskins, eating bread and thinking about being on their way. Even Epifanio's warning could not dampen their spirits for long. Already the animals had more food and water than they would have had at the Roca Estancia, Martin thought. They had not lost a horse. There were no vultures circling overhead here. The parched pampa lay behind them. It lay ahead too, but here there was water, at least enough for one day. There was a morning breeze, rustling the lead mare's bells.

But the wind would not last, and the sky was already a dull, hot blue. They had better get to sleep while they could.

Carlos was already asleep. He was still sitting up, holding his bread, and his mouth lay open for the next bite.

"We'll just pull this *palo borracho*, this drunken log, over to the willows and he'll be all right," Alonso said, taking his younger brother's arm.

"It is already too hot for me to sleep," Martin said as they dumped Carlos in the shade. That was the last thing he remembered.

The next thing he knew, it was late afternoon.

Danger Stalks the Pampa

It was sunset. The hot sky was flooded with crimson behind them and washed thick gray before them. It would be dark in half an hour, and they must move with nightfall. In the desert the insects and animals and night birds did the same. The night before had been like driving a herd through an enormous swarm of bugs. Martin looked over at Carlos barbecuing steaks. Under the perspiration, his face was a mass of mosquito bites.

Martin struggled to act relaxed as he curried Marta's glossy chestnut coat. No time to do more than talk to her today. But that was an important part of the Indian training—to make a horse trust her trainer.

"You're petting her as if she were a kitten," Alonso

85

complained.

"That's the new method! We have kittens instead of horses," Epifanio said, walking up to the fire and sniffing the aroma of the steaks.

"Can we watch the herd well enough from here?" Alonso asked anxiously.

"*Sí.*"

"Is it ready? When do we eat?" Alonso asked. Carlos wagged his finger before his brother's face to show he must wait just a bit longer.

"This is *not* any new method," Martin blurted out with such ferocity that everyone turned in surprise. "I want to train Marta like the Indians train horses. Without the quirt and the whip."

"Train her to do what?" Alonso asked. Epifanio said nothing.

"I don't want a polo pony. I want a horse that can stop in a stride and start again with a flick of my hand and spin with a twitch of my rein if needed. I don't care what color a horse is, but it should be able to handle as well in a bog, on a mountain, or in sand as it does in open pampa."

"In other words, he wants a one-man horse," Alonso said.

"No, an Indian horse behaves as well for a complete stranger." Martin's fury was spent now, and his face was curiously white under his dust coating. He wished he hadn't said anything. Epifanio and Alonso had a right to express their opinions, after all.

"*A la cena*, come to dinner," Carlos said softly, but no one moved. They were waiting for Epifanio to say what he thought. Martin was openly spurning his help by choosing the Indian training. Martin stroked Marta steadily as he waited.

"Put Marta out to pasture. Carlos says it is time for asado," was all Epifanio would say. Was there a pride or pleasure in his voice, or was Martin just wishing? He did not sound angry at least. Neutral. Wait and see? If so, Martin was sure he could show that the method worked.

The boys fell on the dinner with a fury of nervous energy left over from the explosion that hadn't exploded. Martin brought his uncle a heaping plateful of steak and galleta bread, which the old gaucho received with a gracious bend of his head. He sat on a rock outcropping a little apart from the others.

He balanced his plate on one knee and leaned his maté drinking elbow on the other, spearing the meat with his knife. He wore his usual dusty black bombachas and white shirt cinched at the waist with his three inch black leather belt. On his head perched the inevitable flat-topped felt gaucho hat, a cross between a derby and a sombrero. He said nothing, and it seemed impossible to guess what he was thinking. Finally he beckoned to Martin. "Segundo, it is sometimes said that there is more than one way to skin a goat. Let us hope this is true."

"I need to try my way," Martin answered.

"Yours?"

"Well, the Indian way."

Epifanio finished his steak. Then he said quietly enough so only Martin would hear. "*Bueno*, so long as it does not interfere with my drive."

"It will not, Domador." Martin was horrified that his uncle should think it would. Any fool knew the drive must come first.

"If only I had cream for my coffee," Alonso groaned.

Carlos pulled out a small jar labeled "Dairy Cream" in gold letters. The boys had never seen this before and crowded around while he dumped some in Alonso's coffee and stirred. Like magic, coffee with cream. Even Epifanio came over to look and returned to his rock, shaking his head.

"Mama gave me this as a surprise for you, Alonso. A friend brought it to her from the United States." Alonso threw a kiss for the Doña Sulenita at the rancho.

Martin looked over toward the herd. They were walking, scrounging in the dust, starting up, testing their legs and their voices, and playfully chasing one another—gamboling. It was a little cooler now, and they wanted to play. Martin watched the proudly arching necks, high flicking tails, the delicately supple carriage, and thought that Arabians were the most beautiful as well as hardiest horses in all the world. And these were the finest Arabians in all Argentina.

They cavorted now against the red sunset, an omen for clear weather tomorrow. Time to go.

Epifanio looked at the crimson sky. "It is time to start. After one more cup of coffee—or maté," he added, as Alonso passed him the maté.

"This red sky reminds me of the first time I crossed this pampa," the old gaucho went on softly, as if he were talking to himself. "I was just a boy then, about the age of Carlos, though like Martin I was already a segundo. Things were wilder then, but the pampa was much the same: there was drought and the grass was stunted and white too early—as it is tonight. But it is of the sky that I speak now. There were a dozen of us, ten men, myself and one other boy; and we were driving more than two times this many horses. But they were not Arabians, who stick together. No, these were wild horses from the pampa. And we were not the only men who favored these moros. You have never seen so many black horses, so many moros, in one herd. Anyway a tribe of Indians had been following us for days. Just following. It wouldn't have been so bad if they had shown themselves and fought it out man to man in the open. But that wasn't their way. They trailed a Christian until he was so jumpy he couldn't think how to aim his knife, and then one night they swept down on him and left him for the buzzards without his ever having a chance to defend himself or make his peace with God. They would take the horses, after he'd done the work of bringing them across the wide pampa, and drive them into their nearest village.

"Well, this particular night we were half frightened to death but determined this wouldn't happen to us. The red sky told us this was the night. Even though I was but a boy, I looked out over those flashing black horses and knew I couldn't let them go if it meant my life. So we drank enough maté for a hundred men to keep us awake and tried to figure their number. Fifty or more, to judge from shadows we saw now and again against the sky. We lay down and pretended to sleep, our horses tethered near. But as as they crept down toward us, about one in the morning, expecting an easy kill, one of our number crept around behind and began picking them off, so silently none knew there were a dozen fewer. Evening the odds, so to speak. Then we sprang to our horses when they were within a dozen yards and couldn't run away on foot. We made short work of it. Within an hour it was all over but the burying. It was my first taste of battle, right here on the pampa, near this very spot, but it wasn't to be my last by a long shot.

"This is just to let you know this is rugged country. We'll meet no Indians tonight. But, Lord knows, this pampa is full of surprises. *Vamos!*" he added, dumping his maté leaves on the fire. Epifanio methodically washed his plate and packed his few belongings in his saddlebag.

"And I was complaining about a few aches and

pains," Carlos said.

"I, too, had been complaining of aches and pains that very day, as the Indians trailed us step for step, not knowing I would learn the use of the knife before the night was over." Epifanio turned and smiled at Carlos. He motioned for the others to put out the fire and get the herd on the road.

"Now, before we head out tonight," Epifanio said once they were saddled and mounted, "keep a sharp eye out for what lives here, especially our friend the puma. It's been a hard, lean year, and he is hungry. If you see one let *me* know. Above all, don't try to take care of him and don't frighten the herd. And keep an ear out for the cry of a horse taken by surprise. He might be bitten by a snake. I've seen snakes bite under cover of night. Understood?"

The boys nodded.

"Then, *vamos!*"

There was an extra verve and extra snap to the whips and the yells as the boys roused the herd and got them moving that night. It was as if they felt the pampa within them, after knowing what had gone on there.

It was black by the time they were settled into the rhythm of the drive, a trot since it would be a long night. The stars were brightening, and the occasional light of an isolated farmhouse twinkled like home.

Alonso dusted off his harmonica and played a slow tango.

Cuando tu pasas
Coquetona por las calles
Ripiqueteando tu taquito
En la vereda . . .

They sang above the drumlike accompaniment of
hoofbeats. They sang of bad crops and broken hearts
and the evil fates that plague a poor man trying to
care for his family. They sang all the old songs they
had heard from people who could no longer remember when or where they first heard them. Some still
told of fighting to wrest a living from the cruel soil
of Spain. Martin, Epifanio, and Carlos sang these
tangos as if they had been born knowing them. But
as night deepened, they gradually grew silent. Alonso
drew closer to Carlos, talked a moment, and circled
back to the front of the herd.

Martin watched as Carlos turned and galloped back
to him. They rode silently for a while. Finally Martin
broke the silence. "*Qué pasa, amigo*—what is it?
There must be something on your mind besides the
thistles we're riding through and the tons of salve it
is going to take to repair the rips they are giving the
horses."

"The mosquitoes are eating me alive. They think I
am filet mignon. And you know, Martin, I'm cold.
For the first time in months I'm cold."

Carlos sounded miserable. It *was* cold. Martin had
been feeling something strange and could not place

it. So now he knew. He was cold too. He pulled two ponchos from his saddlebag and handed one to Carlos.

When had it turned cold? It had been hot and sticky when they started. Martin realized they'd been gradually climbing up into the foothills all night. There were outcroppings of rock now, and thistle and mesquite bushes were muffling the hoofbeats instead of pampa grass. Ahead loomed the mountains, like a dark impossible wall. Martin shivered.

"*Gracias, amigo,* and now that I am warm I remember Alonso's message. He says to watch for puma. He thought he caught the glint of two sets of eyes."

"Puma! Shuma! Alonso has puma on the brain. Puma doesn't come down to the pampa. Alonso just doesn't want Epifanio to be the only one with adventures on this stretch." Martin spoke with more assurance than he felt. On the one hand, Alonso would just love to feel he had seen a puma. It would be almost as exciting as the polo field. On the other hand, a puma might well come down to foothill water holes because of the drought. This was the season when a mother mountain lion needed the most food for her cubs. But Carlos was not the one to do something about it. He had neither facón nor gun and wouldn't be able to use them if he had. There was no sense in scaring the wits out of him.

"I don't know. . . . The horses are restless. Have you noticed, Martin, when the horses are restless it is as if we were fighting them?"

"Each and every one! Except Gatito," he added. "He handles as well as the best of my uncle's experienced moros."

"Almost," he whispered to himself as Gatito stumbled slightly.

"Are you really going to train Marta like an Indian pony even though she isn't yours?" Carlos asked.

"My uncle didn't say I couldn't, did he?"

"No. But it's so much work for a horse you won't be able to keep. And you will get too fond of her."

Martin shrugged. He didn't mind the work, but he knew Carlos was right about caring too much for her. He already did. But what could he do? Drive her into the herd just because she wasn't his? Carlos shrugged also. He understood. They turned their attention to the horses.

There was no problem with stragglers now. The herd huddled together and Martin heard the high neigh of fear. He could sense fear, running through the horses like electricity. There was some danger near. Though there had been no sign of the big cat, some menace lurked in the thistles and low manzanita bushes. Martin had only a short knife. It would be enough if he could get a good aim.

"Have you seen him?" Martin asked.

"I don't know."

"What do you mean, you don't know? You either see a puma or you don't," Martin said, exasperated.

The horses huddled; their tails were down, tucked between their legs, a sure sign of danger. And their ears were twitching. Mothers were nudging colts to the center of the herd. Even the hoofbeats were lighter now, less certain. What was it Epifanio had said to do? Nothing? That couldn't be right. Martin couldn't remember anything clearly; his mind felt blank.

There were pumas or something even worse close, no question about it. And Carlos would be about as much help as a baby. If only Epifanio knew. Oh, he must sense something. He must! He and Alonso probably felt they couldn't leave their posts; none of them could. There was no sense in presenting the big cat with a colt on a silver platter.

"But a puma won't attack us—isn't that what you said?" Carlos quavered. "What I mean Martin—what I meant is that I saw four eyes—just eyes. It was like they were coming at me in a nightmare!"

"Sounds like it might be a small one, or maybe two cubs. Even a full-grown one would probably only go after the colts. They're supposed to like the way humans smell. How do you smell tonight, Carlos?"

"Like mosquito repellent."

"You're safe. Epifanio once told me a puma stood guard over a wounded gaucho friend of his all night and even chased off a jaguar. Besides, we're moving too fast I think—" Martin stopped short. "Holy Mother of God," he said.

He turned his head away and then back again. They were there all right. Four eyes. Just eyes. The night blackened around them. Over to the left. Carlos saw them, too. About a hundred yards, not more, and coming closer. Slowly. Slowly. Luminous green eyes, bodiless, flowing toward them. Right for them. Right for him. He could not look away, could not scream; for the love of Jesus he hoped he would not scream and cause those eyes to spring. He felt hypnotized. If only he had a facón. He had only one short knife. There were two of them. What did you do when there were two of them?

How much longer before they would spring? Why didn't Carlos do something? At least turn and run while there was still time. They were moving in for the kill now. No question about that. Who would it be? A colt? Carlos? Him? Who? Who? Who?

Without thought or moving more than the one arm, he silently pulled out the whip, lifting it off the saddle horn noiselessly and then snapping it! Snapping it! Snapping it again and again and again. The tears ran down his face, and he shouted to the puma, "There, there, take that! Kill me, will you? What do you think of that?"

Dimly he heard Carlos yelling to him to stop. Stop? How could Carlos ask him to stop? If Epifanio didn't protect them, he had to, didn't he? Where were the pumas? If he stopped, wouldn't they come back? Wouldn't he see those eyes again? The tears streamed down his face as he kept snapping the whip. Suddenly, he felt a whip snap out and catch his, pulling it out of his hand.

"Look at the horses, you crazy fool!" Epifanio yelled as he grabbed hold of Gatito's bridle. "It's just by the grace of God that they haven't stampeded. If you'd been riding the mare, she'd have gone loco. You've lost us the cats with that fool whip of yours.

Why didn't you follow instructions? Is this the Indian method for catching pumas? Stampede the herd, is it? You could have killed us all. Now that wild mother and her cub will trail us forever. They're not the fool you are! They won't leave a soft touch like us as long as there's a colt left." Epifanio hardly paused for breath, rolling out his fury like profanity, without giving one word more importance than any other.

"He did the only thing he could!" Carlos yelled. "The horses are all right."

Martin looked dully at the horses. They clung together like frightened sheep, bleating. They looked as if they had wilted.

"Well, say something. Justify yourself!" Epifanio said. His fury was gone now. He sounded tired. Martin said nothing; it seemed to him he felt nothing, nothing at all.

"We had nothing but one short knife apiece. What could we use but the whips? There was no time to tell you," Carlos said.

"Once or twice, maybe, to frighten them down to my end of the herd, but Martin must have thought he was in the circus. Well, all's well that ends well," he said and reached over to pat Martin on the arm. Martin slapped away his uncle's hand.

"You'd rather the puma got us, is that it?" he said venomously, and burst into tears.

"Are you a boy or a segundo?" Epifanio asked quietly. "A segundo," he went on, "may make many mistakes but he does not resent criticism. He keeps his sorrow to himself."

"So impartially given," Martin said. But the tears stopped. He sat straight.

Epifanio shrugged. He handed Martin a pistol. "If you *must* be a hero, next time use this." He turned quickly and wheeled his horse back to the end of the herd.

"He wouldn't have shouted at *you*," Martin said, "He did not give *me* the gun, either."

Martin said nothing. He felt sick and ashamed. He knew he could have stampeded the horses. And to cry!

"Carlos," he said after a while. "He thinks I disobeyed him on purpose, but I just forgot what he said to do. Those puma eyes!"

"*Sí*, they hold you, the eyes of the puma; but they will not return tonight. It is almost dawn, amigo."

Martin found no comfort in the puma's absence. She was still out there and he knew it. He felt the cold, metallic butt of the pistol. He was amazed that Epifanio had given it to him. He knew how to use it because Epifanio had been teaching him for years. But it was odd. Perhaps, after all, his uncle did have some faith in him. He felt he did not deserve it. He and Carlos rode on in silence.

The Storm

MARTIN WOKE WITH A DEFINITE FEELING THAT THIS was a day to stay asleep. It was cold. The wind blew and the sky was dark. He could not guess what time it was. A heaviness hung over everything. A storm. There was going to be a storm. When a storm came to the mountains, the animals burrowed underground, the birds fought their way to the center of the thickest bush, the flowers closed their petals, and the wind tried to blow a man to the edge of the foothills.

The puma? Where was she? Had he killed her? Martin sat bolt upright. He saw Epifanio sitting by the fire mending a lasso.

"Are we going to have a storm? What time is it? Where is everybody?" he called, awake now.

"We have just finished lunch. There is asado here for you." Epifanio brought him coffee and set about filling his plate. Martin was starving.

"But why was I allowed to sleep when everyone else had to get up?" Martin asked suspiciously. Only children were given special favors. Was he considered a child again?

"We all slept late. Tonight will be hard."

Gradually he remembered the night before: the whip, the pumas, everything. He felt sick—but he was no longer angry. His uncle was right. But that meant he must kill the pumas. They were out there, somewhere, waiting for him. What had to be done had to be done.

"What are you doing?" he asked to change the subject. His uncle had a whole pile of lassos.

"Tonight you need to know how to lasso and throw the boleadoras," the old gaucho answered cryptically.

"We do know!"

Epifanio raised one eyebrow and waved both arms for Carlos and Alonso to come in from the herd. "Eat quickly," he advised Martin. He stood with his arms crossed on his chest, looking up at the sky. No one on the ranch or on the neighboring estancias knew what the sky was thinking with more certainty than he. He shook his head.

"We will go," he said when the two rode up. "Our only chance to keep the herd intact is to reach the first mountain pass where they will have no place to go if they panic when the storm breaks. I had thought to show you a trick or two, something useful when a storm comes. But—there is no time," he added, as suddenly his rope shot out and bound Martin securely around both feet, tripping him and holding him as securely as a calf.

"*Burro!*" Martin yelled angrily.

"But you knew all about roping," Epifanio answered in mock surprise. "Perhaps there are one or two little details you have yet to learn?"

He pulled on the rope, dragging Martin a foot or so. Martin struggled to free himself, though he had seldom seen a calf escape his uncle.

"Shall we take him this way?" Epifanio asked Alonso and Carlos.

"Go to the devil!"

"No," Carlos decided. "We need him to help box the horses in the pass."

Alonso nodded his head in agreement. Epifanio freed Martin with another flick of the wrist and Martin scrambled up, smiling. Somehow, the lassoing meant he was accepted again.

"The storm throws a faster lasso than I—and always when a man is not looking. No one knows *anything* in a mountain storm. We can lose the whole herd in ten minutes unless we work together, and perhaps even then. Be careful!"

"How long do we ride to reach the pass?" Alonso

asked, above the urgent whistle of the wind.

"With the wind behind us, two hours. *Nos vamos?*"

The boys scurried about, putting out the fire, packing or stuffing plates and knives and forks into saddlebags. Martin was saddling Marta when his uncle came up and shook his head.

"Gatito tonight," he said.

Without a word Martin took off the saddle and slapped Marta's rump, sending her back into the herd. He turned and searched out Gatito because his whistle would not be heard above the wind. He saddled the stallion without a backward glance at either his uncle or the mare.

Ten minutes later they were off. It did not take much urging to get the horses moving. It would have been another story if they had had to buck the wind, but as it was, the wind fairly blew them along. The horses tucked their tails between their legs and set off at a full gallop. The boys rode crouched over their saddles; but Epifanio sat stiff as a ramrod, defying a mere wind to make him bend *his* back. Even when the hail he predicted fell on that back, he would do no different. The hail would break instead.

Dust blew in little cyclones around them. It got stronger, worse and yet worse. The boys rode with kerchiefs tied over their noses like bandits, driving the horses on to the possibility of shelter. The horses still tucked their tails between their legs, laid their ears forward, and set their heads straight ahead. They snorted to blow the dust from their nostrils. And kept moving. There was a determination in the set of the herd, a grim resolve not to stop until they had somehow evaded both wind and dust. There was no turning back or aside. The wind saw to that.

Martin rode Gatito tonight, a horse with experience. Somewhere in that swirling mass Marta shivered. This would be her first storm. What would she do?

Martin felt also some greater terror hovering behind or above the wind. Was this just because he knew of the possible rain? Did the horses feel this too? Could they sense rain and hail? Did they *know*, while he just guessed?

This was rocky foothill country, not steep enough for contained passes but uneven enough to keep the horses stumbling almost continually. It was certainly no place to meet a storm! If a hailstone didn't get a horse coming down, it would break a leg rebounding off a loose rock. The horses would scatter in all directions; only luck would save even half the herd. It was only six o'clock but almost dark. Normally there would be another three hours of light this time of the summer. And the dust! The horses might stampede if this went on. Who knew what two hundred and fifty thirsty Arabians might do when fed nothing but dust for a day and a night?

With luck they could have reached the Condor Inn on the edge of the great Pampa Achala tonight, where the horses could have their fill of water and high moist grass. But luck did not include a storm. Nor pumas. What would the horses do, when they were already about to bolt if they smelled a puma?

Martin was suspended, held in the dust and the dark. He could see no one, could hear nothing but hoofbeats and the howling air, could feel nothing but dust that caked him inside and out. Yet, he had to be constantly on the lookout for stray branches or trees now. He envied the horses, who thought they could avoid the dangers of darkness by just lowering their heads.

What was that? Martin felt something packed and solid beneath Gatito's hoofs. A road? It was too good to be true! It was probably only a dirt road, but at least until it rained they could travel fast and safely. The horses stretched out in a long shaggy line three or four or four-and-a-colt abreast with the men patrolling the edges. The whips were cracking constantly now. Everything was at a full gallop. They would be in the pass soon, but soon enough? Martin could not tell. The sky was unknown above the dust storm.

He tried to keep track of Marta's golden chestnut coat. He could pick her out from time to time by her curious habit of pulling to the left as she galloped, occasionally bumping another horse. He could tell she was frightened. This was a time of terror for all of them.

It was hard to tell who was most anxious to gallop on to safety, the humans or the horses. Carlos rode alongside Martin briefly.

"And this was all your idea. Don't forget that!" Carlos yelled through wind and hoofbeats.

"Still better than dying of thirst," Martin called back. His voice echoed eerily against the bare hills.

"Oh, we may do that too, before we're done! Oh-oh, the wind is dropping. It won't be long now. Here she comes."

"We must be almost there. The mountains look high enough on either side now to make a horse think twice about clambering up."

"*Vamos muchachos!*" Epifanio called. "*Pronto! Prontisimo!* To the ends of the herd. Cut off the escape! *Muchachos . . .*" What else Epifanio might have said was cut off by a flash of lightning and a clap of thunder. This was it! Carlos dashed toward one end and Martin toward the other to help Alonso.

For a moment the sky blazed and thundered like a roll of drums. The lead mare's bell beat a ghostly counterpoint, an uneven frightened tinkle. Horses and men paused, waiting. Then it came. Not rain, hail! Hailstones the size of walnuts, then hailstones the size of small apples pelted them as the heavens opened up. It felt like the end of the world, as if a gigantic landslide were inundating them. And beyond the mountains the pampa wasn't getting a drop of water. This was a local storm, a mountain fury. It might kill them all and be no help to anyone.

"But it will not kill us, not if I can help it. Easy Gatito, easy *pobre*."

Horses squealed and gave one horribly long, shrill cry that echoed through the canyon. They were stunned for a moment like statues. This was the moment Martin needed to work Gatito to the canyon opening. He reared and snorted, but Martin kept a firm grip on the reins. After a moment he was perfectly docile. Perhaps he thought Martin was a better hope than the wild commotion now going on to every side of them. Gatito trusted him.

Horses pawed the ground, dashed to the side of the canyon only to be thrown back by its steep quartz face. Martin couldn't be sure, but some seemed to be getting footholds and going up. Foals were trampled. Any horse that fell was sure to be trampled to death.

Through it all, Martin could hear Epifanio wildly cracking his whip, riding here, there, and everywhere like a wild man keeping the horses in line, slowing them, picking them from the foaming mass, and calling his own name incessantly.

"E-pi-fan-i-o, E-pi-fan-i-o Gui-men-ez! E-pi-fan-i-o Gui-men-ez!" He called to let them know where he was, as he risked his life every second to save the herd of Arabians. How could Martin and Alonso do less? The hailstones bounced on the dry hard ground around them and hit them again on the rebound.

The horses grew panicky! If only it would rain! Hooves slipped and slid on the hailstones. Horses fell under other horses and their shrieks filled the night. Martin no longer knew what happened or what he was doing as he dashed about helping horses. There was no light except the flashes of lightning. He could orient himself only by Epifanio's call.

He thought he saw Marta dash up the sheer cliff and slip back during one flash. Did she cry? Was that her? Had she slipped off her feet for the one fatal instant? There was an entire herd between them and no possibility of finding out.

"Marta! Marta!" Martin gasped.

Epifanio's voice stopped in the middle of a triumphant bellow of his name. Martin strained to hear the rest. Had it been lost in the maelstrom? Why didn't he call again? Where was he? Had he been trampled —too? From what direction had the last call come? Martin strained to remember. . . . Over to the left. That was it, over to the left. Near where Marta had been.

Alonso was somewhere near, too, rounding up foals so they would not be trampled.

"Epifanio! Epifanio!" Martin yelled at the top of his lungs, tears and sweat cutting rivulets through the dust caking his face. No answer. He saw Carlos. At least he still lived.

The hail stopped suddenly. And the rains poured. The sky seemed to be an overturned bucket. The horses might get pneumonia, but at least they were quiet. They understood rain. It was to be waited out. They stood quietly now, and Martin was sorely tempted to climb under Gatito's belly and sit there, relatively dry, until the rains stopped. But he had to find Epifanio.

"Carlos! Alonso! Have you seen Epifanio or Marta?"

"What the hell do you think *I'm* looking for?" Alonso answered. So he had heard the unfinished cry too.

"What happened? Where is Epifanio?" Carlos asked, reining in his horse close to Martin. The rain poured on them as if they were under a waterfall.

"The last I heard he was right in the middle of the herd, yelling like crazy," Martin bellowed over the roar of the rain.

"Well, at least the rain is better than dust. We can see. I've been through most of the herd and I didn't see him. A tough old gaucho like Epifanio is all right. He's probably riding furiously after some poor horse that thought it could escape him. Martin, do you hear me? I said he's all right."

"He wasn't trampled. I've been all over. He's just not here," Alonso yelled over to them.

"Hey—don't faint—!" Carlos suddenly called over to his brother. "Get down off your horse." Alonso slipped off his horse and stood leaning against it, white and shaken, the rain pelting him.

"You don't look so good yourself." He grinned as Carlos came over to help. "In fact, you and Martin are as knobby as potatoes, only I've never seen black and blue potatoes. Any broken bones?"

The rain was letting up, and they looked at one another. All were covered with welts that were rising and turning black and blue minute by minute. Martin couldn't feel either broken bones or any sensation of pain. He wondered briefly if he were in shock, but then went back to the nagging question of Epifanio. Maybe Epifanio did ride after a strayed horse. But how could he have gotten up that steep quartz cliff? He couldn't have. If anyone could, more of the horses without riders would have tried it.

"Well, we've saved the greater part of the herd," Alonso said. "Epifanio was right about these steep walls. Some got out the ends, but I'd say we were lucky." There was a tired triumph in Alonso's voice. They *had* saved the greater part of the herd, how many it was still impossible to tell. Most of the horses stood placidly in the now gentle rain, enclosed in the steepest, narrowest valley Martin had ever seen. It was really more of a gorge than a canyon. Experienced gauchos usually lost herds in this kind of a freak storm, and they hadn't. They hadn't lost the herd. Martin kept repeating it to himself. But they had saved what they did because Epifanio had known about this bottleneck and had gotten them here in time. The old weathervane, Martin thought proudly.

Got them there with not five minutes to spare.

"I've got to find him—now!" Martin suddenly said, and wheeled Gatito. Alonso caught the bridle and held it fast.

"No! Not before daybreak!"

"Martin, there's not even a moon to see by."

"You couldn't possibly find him before daybreak, and we can't contain the horses—just one on each end. Someone's got to put salve on the herd and build a fire and—He'll probably be back soon, and then he'd have to go out hunting for you."

Alonso's voice was gentle. He seemed to be trying to remember just what they did have to do, and Martin suddenly realized why. Alonso was in charge now! He was responsible with Epifanio gone. He was also right. Martin knew he couldn't find a mountain tonight and that his uncle might well come back by morning. Alonso needed him badly. This was his job. But it was hard, hard not to do something to find Epifanio. He clenched his fists and held himself rigid, unconsciously just as his uncle did. But Epifanio would expect him to stay here and help—would rely on him to do it.

"All right," he said finally, "but I ride at dawn! I think Marta's gone too," he added.

"He'll be back by then," Alonso said, squeezing his arm, "and when he does he'll probably use the lasso on us all if there isn't a fire and we haven't taken care of the horses. Let's see to the fire first."

"With what?" Carlos asked. The rain had stopped, but it was pitch black and nothing would be dry after the rain, even if there were wood in the canyon, which there probably wasn't.

"Epifanio put wood in my saddlebags and packed the burros," Alonso replied.

The fire helped a little. The moon and the stars began to break through after the rain. By their light the boys could count the horses as they sprawled exhausted on the canyon floor. Some shook themselves by rippling muscles that horses alone have under the skin to dry themselves. Others slept where they stood or lay. Their manes hung like dozens of black snakes along their necks. The smell of blood hung over the canyon, dark red blood that ran from every kind of wound and dried black on matted hair.

Though there seemed to be no dead horses, almost a quarter of the herd was missing. And this in spite of the desperate drive to enclose them in the gloomy canyon. The three boys were freezing cold, soaked to the marrow, welts over every inch of their skin from the hail; and still they had to care for the horses before they could sleep. They stood with their backs to the fire, steaming themselves relatively dry.

Martin wondered if Carlos was afraid of the dark again tonight? And if Alonso felt good about being in charge? No, if he could judge by looking at Alonso's gloomy face. Perhaps he was more worried about Epifanio than he admitted. Martin didn't dare let himself think of the possibilities. He thought only of the present. They should get started caring for the horses or they would lose the herd to infection. But somehow he could neither move, nor comfort his friends, nor speak. He could not believe anything serious had happened to his tough uncle, but he could not move either until—until what? Perhaps until the old gaucho was safe. He should have told Epifanio that he understood about riding Gatito instead of Marta tonight. Why had he been silent?

So they stood there warming themselves and not feeling anything. Each knew he should get moving, should see to the horses, dry equipment, prepare for the work he knew was coming. But no one moved.

No one knew how long they stood there before Carlos whispered tensely, "Look, up at the top of that cliff. Tell me if I see what I think I see."

"My God," Alonso whispered too. "Martin?"

"What?"

"Don't move, but just look up to the left—"

'Where?"

"It is—"

"There at the top," Alonso said fiercely.

"Look," Carlos whispered. "Look and tell me if I see what I think I see." He pointed to the crescent of the divide.

"Epifanio!" Martin yelled.

"E-pi-fan-i-o!" came the reply, loud and clear.

"Epifanio Guimenez!" they shouted together, waving their hats and slapping each other on the back, as if redeemed from some evil spell.

"Why, the old devil," Alonso said admiringly.

"Thank God," Martin said. "How did he do it?"

"How?"

"I knew he'd be back."

Epifanio stood on the very top of the divide, astride his horse like an Indian brave. And then, as he started picking his way down the treacherous quartz mountain side, they saw that he was leading a string of horses. How many? Martin scanned them quickly, but Marta was not among them. He was ashamed of himself. That was too much to ask.

"There must be twenty of them!"

"Now he'll tell us he can handle the herd alone even when there *is* a stampede. We'll never, never live *this* down," Carlos whispered happily.

"Put on some water for maté."

"I'll curry our horses."

"We'd better put the salve on or at least get started, or he'll skin us alive," Martin said.

"Gatito, he's back! He's back," Martin whispered over and over to his stallion as he curried him gently. "Wait until I tell him how well *you* did tonight."

Suddenly and for no reason, since he could see by moonlight that she was not among the horses, Martin cupped his hands to his mouth and called out, "Did you find Marta?"

He could have bitten off his tongue. He had meant

to tell his uncle how worried he'd been and how glad he was to see him, but somehow this—accusation came out instead. Martin could see that Carlos and Alonso were shocked. So was he.

"Martin, I will." The promise broke the still night as the gaucho rode down into the valley and slapped the horses into the sleeping herd. He was soaked to the skin. His back was ramrod straight as ever. He had returned.

Long Day of the Gaucho

THERE WAS NO QUESTION OF EVEN A LITTLE SLEEP that morning, Martin thought ruefully as he ate cold crackers for breakfast. They huddled around a meager campfire, worn from a night of storm and work, prolonging a cup of coffee until sunrise when they all knew they must get on with their job. They were still short almost a fifth of the herd, even counting the horses Epifanio had brought in. Every horse had scratches and bruises to be poulticed, disinfected, and watched anxiously for infection. Some were done, but more remained. Fortunately the day promised to be mild and warm, so the danger of pneumonia was lessened.

But a good day also meant it would be hard to contain the horses in the steep quartz canyon, the canyon Doña Marta had called "pickle pass" because of its shape and color. When Martin looked out the narrow end of the pass, he saw only more stubble and rocks, but he knew the horses would soon feel any grass they saw was greener than what they had. He only hoped they were as tired as he was.

And then they must move on. Tonight at the latest. For there was no grazing, no water, not even safety in this land of the puma and the vulture and the snake. They must limp away, leaving stray horses to almost certain death. They had only today to find them, before the drive went on to the lush, high Pampa Achala where their tails would sweep green grass for almost a hundred miles, and horses and men could rest. There could be no rest here where there was such danger.

"Remember, a horse in the herd is worth two in the brush. We'll keep a split shift, two standing guard and drying out gear and two on roundup. *Entiende*, understand?"

The boys nodded wearily. Finally Alonso stood up. "One thing about this slave driver," he said, putting an arm around Epifanio's shoulder. "He's the only man alive who can build a fire of rock instead of wood."

"And I would not have built it at all if I knew you planned to sit telling tales like tough old hens all the long day!" Epifanio replied crossly. He stood holding all the lassos.

"Last night is not exactly ancient history. You don't go through a storm like that every day in the year," Carlos complained.

"A man does not spend three hours talking of one hour's work. *Vamos*. Every horse we do not find today—poof." Epifanio clapped his hands expressively.

No one moved.

"All right. Let us all sit like lawyers. More maté, please. Marta will understand." Epifanio sat with his back turned to the fire.

"But I am not a lawyer yet, so I still work," Carlos said meekly as he stood up and started spreading out gear to dry.

Epifanio said nothing. When he finally turned, it was to speak to Martin who had not said a word all morning.

"Eh, Martin?"

"Martin, Martin, cat got your tongue? You haven't said one word all morning!" Carlos sounded worried.

"Epifanio, why the lassos? Going to lasso Martin again?" Alonso asked.

Epifanio clucked his tongue and waved his finger in front of Alonso's nose. "No. This is for a little lesson. If we meet stray horses, I want you to be able to keep them."

"Oh, no!" Alonso groaned.

But Martin nodded and stood up. He was ready for the lesson, though he hadn't the energy to speak.

When he was very tired—and he had never been so tired in his whole life—conversation seemed useless to him. He saw his uncle look over sympathetically and felt he understood. Epifanio was famous for his silences. Martin smiled at the old gaucho. He was ashamed of his outburst last night over one horse when the herd must be rescued. Perhaps Epifanio understood this too.

Then he looked down toward the horses. They seemed none the worse for the storm from a distance. They were cavorting in the rising sun. Two young foals were challenging each other to a race. Others pranced, threw up their heels, and snorted. Maybe they were testing themselves to make sure everything was still in working order. And who could blame them? Only a few nuzzled their wounds, sniffing in annoyance. Martin looked for the peculiar golden chestnut of Marta's sleek coat. He knew she was not there but he looked anyhow. No, she was not there. No one knew where she was. And they had only today to find her.

Epifanio handed each boy a lasso. He stood in front and demonstrated a lightning throw, whistling through the air. Then he pointed for Alonso to follow his example. They were to aim for a point in air. He said air was more elusive than a post and therefore better. Alonso tried but his lasso fell limply. Epifanio frowned and threw his again. It snapped the air abruptly, powerfully, with command.

"Alonso, think as you throw of the death that awaits every horse you do not lasso correctly today, every horse we lose. Will it be eaten by the puma, stung by a snake, or perhaps only die of thirst and provide food for the vultures? This may help you throw!"

Alonso flushed deeply. He was the son of the owner and not used to being spoken to like that. He clenched his teeth and said nothing. This time his lasso ripped the air, cutting it like a knife.

Epifanio nodded. Martin. Carlos. Alonso. Again and again. They kept this up without rest for half an hour. Martin was in agony. Each minute was taking Marta and the other horses farther and farther away. He knew they were somewhere out there and that this practice might make the difference between saving them and not saving them. But enough was enough. Why didn't they ride?

"All right. *Bueno*. Enough. Just remember that the man who has faced the wilderness never jokes about it. Do not joke with the lasso. One more thing. You rode well last night. I could not have controlled the horses without you. I will tell Don Jaime this," Epifanio finished quietly.

The boys stared at him. No one had ever heard Epifanio say anything so nice, so outright complimentary. Martin flushed beet red. Alonso and Carlos shuffled their feet and did not look up. Silently they shook hands with a startled Epifanio and with Martin.

Then they let out a bellow to match Epifanio's own.

"Ep-i-fan-i-o!" the brothers yelled in unison. It was enough to split the eardrums the first time and then it echoed back more shrilly from each canyon wall. Epifanio held his head.

"*Idiotas!* Fools, you'll stampede the horses. *Basta!*" This also echoed so eerily that even Epifanio laughed. "I was about to add," he went on finally in a whisper, "I was about to add that you must do better today. We leave at sundown. Carlos and Alonso, you will stay and care for the horses. Salve, poultice, and remember that a horse is an animal that has touchy feelings and a lot of sense. Oh, dry our gear. Martin, we'll ride the first shift after the mavericks," he said over his shoulder as he mounted his black stallion. Martin whistled for Gatito.

"We'll be back by noon, no matter what. Do not leave the horses alone. If you hear a stray nearby, one of you go—Alonso is better with the lasso, so he goes —but not the two. *Entiende?* Always remember a horse in the herd is—"

"Worth two in the brush," Carlos finished.

Martin turned Gatito so that he followed Epifanio's impatient black stallion. He could see that his uncle was amused by Carlos's teasing. How did either of them have the wit or the energy? He felt as if he were riding in his sleep, except that every bone in his body ached. At least he would not have to talk with his uncle. They sometimes passed a whole day together without speaking. They had lived together so long that words often seemed unnecessary. They understood each other. They rode on in silence perhaps an hour, each scanning the horizon. Epifanio sniffed as if he could smell the horses he sought. Martin wondered how he had decided which direction to take. Had he seen Arabians head this way last night?

Did Epifanio feel they had lost too many horses? That was a useless question. For Epifanio, even losing one horse was a personal defeat. They rode side by side now. Epifanio's shirt sleeves were rolled up to the elbow, and he was completely black and blue.

"Old men bruise easily," Martin said finally, indicating the arm. Epifanio rolled down first one shirt sleeve and then the other without comment. They were silent again. It was getting hot. The rocks were steaming out the last of the storm. This was rocky foothill country below the pickle pass and there was no sign of any life.

"Do you hunt the herd or only the mare?" Epifanio asked after a while.

Martin blushed. He knew that his uncle rotated his four black stallions without preference. And Marta was not even Martin's own horse. What could he say? Epifanio did not understand caring for one horse above all the others. And Martin understood why now. For the domador, the welfare of the herd must come or he would soon have no herd at all.

"Perhaps we will find her," the gaucho said gently.

"Aha!" he went on before Martin had a chance to answer. "Chewed grass. And the stubble beaten down. Many horses. Finally we have a little luck, eh?"

"Grass?" A dry moss covered the rocks but there wasn't enough in a mile to fodder a horse. What there was, however, had been yanked and pulled and chewed. The horses must be starving!

"Well, we'll have pampa grass and feather pillows tonight," Martin said.

"Maybe," Epifanio answered laconically.

"Maybe? You said we had to leave by sundown, and Doña Marta told us the Condor Inn is only three hours' ride from the pickle pass!" Martin didn't like the hesitation in his uncle's voice.

"It is never good to count on feather beds," was all Epifanio would say.

Just then Martin saw them. There were a dozen, no, there were fifteen horses milling about nearly halfway up the far embankment. The sun reflected on their rain-washed coats. They were grubbing for the dry moss. Martin pulled at Epifanio's sleeve.

"Ah, there they are! If only your Gatito does not greet them, we may have some luck. Too many for the lassos. Skittish but hungry. We could use another man. *No importa*, it doesn't matter. You ride to the left and I will cover on the right. Straight out to the pass."

Martin nodded.

"Now, *vamos*."

Martin galloped to the rear of the horses where they would not catch his scent. He waited until his uncle had circled wide around and then at a signal bore down on the wanderers. While he yelled and snapped his whip, he wondered if scaring them was necessary. After all, these were horses he brought down from the pasture every morning. They should know him. But Epifanio had been right about so many things on the drive, that Martin did what he said without arguing.

Martin saw immediately that Marta was not among them. He felt a sinking in the pit of his stomach. Then he went to work. The strays were neighing and whinnying but docile. In truth they offered no resistance. Martin policed one side and Epifanio the other, keeping the pace to a gallop. It was important to get the horses back to camp before they had time to think about it.

They covered passes, hills, and valleys with the hollow ring of hoofs against rock echoing in Martin's ears. Horses and men were covered with sweat. Martin didn't know what he would use for a horse if he went out on another hunt with Epifanio. He couldn't take Gatito again. And Marta was lost. He scanned the horizon for the mare, but the horizon was empty.

His uncle was scanning the sky. "There is time yet. We have been out only three hours and found fifteen horses. The gaucho asks only for a long day."

Martin groaned. He liked a long day, but it seemed

that all his life whenever he'd been completely exhausted, his tireless uncle had asked only for a longer day. The everlasting long day of the gaucho.

Martin was hardly conscious when they rode into camp. Dimly he heard the strays join the herd with glad whinnies. Dimly he heard Alonso say a few horses had returned. Gatito must have stopped of his own accord. Good old friend.

"Maté?" he heard Alonso whisper. And then, "Epifanio, he's asleep in the saddle. Help me get him down?"

"I am not asleep. All I need is some maté," he heard himself say indignantly.

The next thing Martin knew someone was shaking him.

"Hey! Leave me alone."

"*Perezoso*, lazy one. Help me fix dinner. It's almost time to go."

"Time to go? Time to go? I've got to find Marta. Why did you let me sleep? We've got to save her from the puma!" Martin started up wildly, clinging to Carlos, still only half awake.

"*Amigo*, take it easy. Alonso is out hunting for Marta now. You were half dead, and we still have a hard ride tonight."

"Only three hours, Doña Marta said."

"But she also said every step we'd have to fight holes, snakes, and loose rock."

"You know it seems as if we've been every step of

this trip before. I hear Doña Marta talking as I ride along. Strange," Carlos said.

"Why strange?"

"That she could have known *so* much from books. Oh, Alonso and the weathervane found three more horses. The hard way, one by one. He said to tell you that if we get started two or three hours before sundown we can cover all the terrain before us where they might have strayed," Carlos said matter-of-factly.

"Well, let's go! What are we waiting for? Where's Epifanio?"

Carlos pointed to Epifanio, who was sitting by a fire in the heat of the day, sound asleep. "I wondered about laying him down, but I was afraid he might not approve. This probably isn't the first time he's slept sitting up."

Martin smiled and shook his head. No, it was not the first time.

"He told me," Carlos went on, "that the whole storm lasted less than an hour!"

"Oh, Carlos! Epifanio is teasing. We were at it all night." Martin was quickly gathering gear as he talked.

"*Amigo*, no. He is right, I think. *Sí* all this work and the herd battered in an hour. Twenty-one horses still missing. Mother Nature is *una loca mujer*, no?"

"Twenty-one still missing and Epifanio sleeps?" Martin was astounded.

Carlos stopped stuffing maté leaves into the pot and

turned. "He did not sleep today. He scouted for hours after you slept, hunting for your precious Marta. And as you see, he does not sleep willingly now."

"How do you know he hunted for Marta?" Martin was deeply ashamed. He had taunted his uncle by asking about the horse when he came riding down the cliff. And then while *he* slept his uncle had gone out hunting for *his* mare.

"I ached too much to sleep or to ride, so I kept the fire going. And is there not something . . . sinister about this canyon?"

"*Sí*, storms, snakes, pumas, starvation, and the ghosts of victims. We can't leave too soon for me. But Epifanio seemed to be having the time of his life last night." Martin smiled, remembering his wild cries.

"Alonso too, after Epifanio came back. But I kept thinking how I will enjoy being a lawyer." The two boys got all the gear packed and the camp ready to break as they talked. Carlos looked relieved as he saw his brother riding toward camp. Now, they could go.

Martin, after noticing that Alonso brought no horses, went back to thinking about Carlos. He knew that Carlos meant exactly what he said. He would be a lawyer. How could they feel so differently? They had been together and done most of the same things every day of their lives. Martin felt as tired as Carlos, but he had never felt so alive, so *vivo*.

"Epifanio thinks Marta panicked and pushed on

ahead. She was terrified when he last saw her. He says
you only backtracked today, so we may still find her
ahead as we ride toward Condor Inn."

"Well, let's get started then." Martin woke Epifanio.

The old gaucho sprang up, lasso ready to throw.
He was horrified. "Where are we? Where's my
mount? What happened?"

"You had a little rest," Carlos said gently.

"You shouldn't have let me sleep, not while the
herd is broken. *Pronto!* We ride. A minute counts an
hour now! *Vamos!* Alonso—no luck?"

The boys found themselves chewing a jerky dinner
as they rode off ten minutes later. The horses were
sluggish and stiff and had to be pushed to get started.
Then a wind came up and brought its quota of dust,
but Epifanio promised it would not bring rain, and
so the boys paid little attention. They had reason to
trust their weathervane, and dust had become a part
of their lives. Their eyes were on the horizon.

It was late in the afternoon now. Long shadows
fell on the rose and green quartz lining the canyon.
They had two, three hours at the most. Night didn't
take its time here in the mountains. It fell like an
apple. And then they would find no more horses.

"Hyiaa!" Epifanio called and was answered by a
high whinny. "The good saints have not forgotten
their poor sinners," he said in astonishment as half a
dozen mares and two colts galloped toward them at

top speed. They joined the herd with much whinnying and shoving, tossing proud heads on lofty necks,
and flaring defiance if another horse failed to give
way. The herd enveloped them without even breaking the cadence.

"Even an *old* gaucho sees something new every
day."

"I just wish they would all come back that way,"
Martin said to his uncle, who had taken off his hat
and was fanning his face as he watched the mares.

"Hmph! It would be no credit to us if they did,"
he said sourly and rode off. Martin knew he felt
cheated of the glory of bringing them in. Maybe
more would come? Maybe—

> Oh, the day is long
> When the night is sad
> And you are far away. . . .

Alonso played a mournful tune on his harmonica
and it matched their mood as they picked their way
up the broad foothill. It was more than an hour,
almost dark, before they saw another horse. They
were feeling tired and hungry, and thinking more of
the feather beds at Condor Inn than the lost horses.
Even Martin had given up. This was going to be their
one comfortable night in a hotel. They would quarter
their horses in a corral and everyone could sleep.

Suddenly Epifanio took off for the top of the

mountain. He seemed to be galloping straight up into thin air. Whatever he had seen, he was going after it, even to the very gates of heaven.

Martin shrugged. He didn't see a thing. What had the old hawk seen? Certainly no *horse* could have gotten up *there*. Look at him go! "Hyiiiia!"

He caught just a glimpse of something brown and moving at the very summit before he heard Epifanio's triumphant cry and saw his rope lash out. Martin thought at first he saw a horse pulled up as usual when that rope flashed out. But, no, the horse had apparently ducked just in the nick of time, for it tore across the ledge now, neighing its own triumphant cry. It was a beauty, smaller and lighter than most, but with the absolute grace and litheness of the pure Arabian. One of the Roca herd, no question about that. It stood for a moment, impatient, quivering. Then they were off again.

Martin gasped. Was it possible? At this distance he could only see a shadow but there was something about the way the horse moved, pulling a little to the left, something about the airy pace that was more floating than galloping that made Martin catch his breath. It must be Marta! There could not be another horse who moved just as she did. It must be Marta. He was sure.

But if that was Marta, then his uncle was all wrong. He could not force her, beat her, or lasso her. She'd been taught to obey because she wanted to. He'd never get her that way. Never. The fool would lose her.

They were galloping straight down the mountain now, right into the rear of the herd. She'd stampede the herd. Alonso wheeled to head them off.

"It's Marta," he yelled over his shoulder.

"I know!" Martin turned and rode toward them. He was too late to reach them in time, he knew, but perhaps he could do something. He watched his horse dodge skittishly as she could see the riders funneling

her in. Blast his uncle! Didn't he remember that this was the horse who threw him? He was going to lose her for good if he wasn't careful. Him and his gaucho training. The horse skirted the herd, edging around as if she might finally make her break for it at the open end of the herd.

And she might have, if Martin hadn't sensed her thinking, and skirted the other side, heading her off. As he did so, he kept whistling for her. This was the way he normally called her, and he was careful to keep it slow and easy, without the urgency he felt. At first she paid no attention and then, gradually, though she didn't seem to lose her gait, her ears lay back. She turned her head. Finally, her gait faltered. She seemed annoyed. She danced now undecided.

Then a strange thing happened. She stopped. Just stood still! Marta stood as if frozen to the spot at the edge of the herd, which was also still now. She did not come toward Martin. Epifanio stood too, just watching. Finally, her head and tail high, she turned and walked into the herd.

"Marta, Marta!" the boy called. He whistled. He was about to ride into the herd after her when his uncle laid a sweaty hand on his arm.

"Let her sleep it off," he advised wearily.

"But she acted as if she didn't even know me," Martin said.

"She knew you or she wouldn't have given up so easily. She had it in her to give us a bit more of a run for our money, that mare," Epifanio assured him and then paused. "But . . . she would rather be free," he added gently.

Martin nodded sadly. He understood, and he felt very close to his uncle for reminding him. Who would not rather be free?

"Thank you for finding her. I had given up," he said shyly, completely forgetting that he had been furious with Epifanio for his strong-arm methods.

"I promised," he replied simply, and then quickly added, "All the gaucho asks is a long day to finish his work."

"Well, it's over now." Martin grinned, indicating the fact that it was almost pitch black.

"No, only dark," Epifanio retorted and gave the signal to start. Snapping of whips and the hollow pounding of a thousand hoofs broke the stillness of the mountain night. And through the clamor Martin heard something else, like a distant echo of another life. Alonso was playing his harmonica.

The Puma

THE NIGHT WAS BLACK. THE MOON WAS STILL BELOW the horizon, and the few early stars only intensified the dark. The horses' heads were down, as they picked their way up the steep mountain paths by instinct. Martin could see nothing. Any horse who wanted to rejoin the herd now would have to find *them*. There was no point in looking. The only eyes anyone would see tonight would be the puma's. And Martin did not feel up to meeting those.

Even the condors slept. Tomorrow perhaps they would see the great birds near the inn that bore their name, the national birds of Argentina. Condor Inn lay at the very top of these mountains, and they should reach it in another hour or two. Thank God.

Tonight he would sleep. And tomorrow he might see condors for the first time outside a zoo. He would see them where they were free to sweep through an entire sky if they wished. With a wingspread of twenty feet, they needed an entire sky!

It wouldn't be long now. Maybe the worst was over. Feather beds ahead.

Martin felt he had been over all the terrain they were covering before, because Doña Marta's geography books had been so complete, her training so thorough. But her pictures of the Condor Inn had completely captured his imagination. He felt he already knew every nook and cranny.

The enormous wooden hotel was perched between the mountain peaks. There was no other house at all for miles around. And all across the front were the widest wooden steps he had ever seen. They were steps that kings and presidents had walked, for this was the most famous inn in all Argentina.

He strained his eyes to see it. Not yet. But it would not be long. How good it would be to get out of the cold. Poor Carlos must be an icicle. Who would have thought it could be so cold just four days' ride from Chepes where they had been sweltering night and day on the estancia.

"Maybe the worst is over, amigo." Alonso said, riding up alongside Martin.

"Alonso! I couldn't see you. I was just thinking the same thing. Maybe we'll get some rest, and I'll have time to train Marta, and the horses will get pampa grass—"

"Do not tempt the fates, Martin! Your uncle sent me to make sure you and Carlos are all right. He says the herd is uneasy."

"Uneasy? Exhausted is probably a better word," Martin said, but he suddenly felt uneasy himself. There *was* something bothering the horses. They seemed to huddle together. It was cold. Maybe they were cold and tired and huddling close for the warmth. Horses did this every winter back on the estancia. What was Epifanio getting so upset about? But even as he reasoned, Martin felt a shiver run up his spine. Fear, not cold.

"Shall I tell Epifanio that you're all right?"

"*Sí*, we are fine. I will tell Carlos."

"*Gracias*. Well, see you at Condor Inn." Alonso wheeled and was lost in the night.

Martin edged over toward Carlos. He scanned the horizon but saw nothing. What Epifanio was thinking just wasn't possible. He was too used to expecting the worst. It just was not possible that after the storm and this devastating day rounding up stray horses they could have anything more to face. Not today!

And yet? Martin's stomach sank. The horses were right. They knew the feel of a mountain lion in the vicinity. They sensed it with an instinct beyond the experience of a boy's lifetime. They were in danger. Martin knew it in their fear and in his own.

"Carlos?"

"*Sí, amigo.*"

"Carlos, I . . . am afraid."

"The puma?"

"*Sí,* how did you know? You always know what I'm thinking. Epifanio says the herd is uneasy."

"I have not seen her, but I think . . . the horses act to me as they did before when pumas were with us. See how they pull their tails between the legs. That is not from the cold, amigo. There is no wind now."

"Her?" How could he know the sex? Carlos must assume it was the same puma still trailing them. The puma they had lost because he was stupid. Martin's hands were clammy and his throat dry. He could not have spoken if his life depended on it. And it might.

They rode on in silence, each trying to peer through the dust and the night. If only the moon would rise. Soon. But it was not yet due. Martin felt his heart beat in time with the frenzied cadence of the herd.

He felt for his pistol and waited. He saw no eyes. But he knew they were there. Somewhere out in the brush. Waiting just as he was waiting. The horses knew it too.

Then Martin saw them. The four eyes. Two higher than the others. That would be the mother and her cub. Just the way they had been before. His pumas! He had a gun. Why hadn't he asked Epifanio if he needed to cock it? You always cocked pistols, didn't you? He couldn't ask Carlos. He felt tongue-tied.

And all the while he watched the eyes, moving slowly and slowly toward them. How far away were they? How close did they get before they sprang? Close and closer. Don't look at them. The thing was not to get hynotized, not to go loco watching those eyes.

Several of the horses gave a high-pitched whinny of warning. They had seen them. Had Carlos? What good would it do? He didn't have a weapon. It was he, Martin, who had the gun.

They were his pumas! His hand fumbled with the gun. The eyes couldn't be more than a hundred yards

away now. There, the pistol was cocked. He pulled it out. Now don't panic. No more shots than necessary. All that was needed was to stampede the horses. No canyon to enclose them here. These were open foothills. Martin was counting as he thought: "one, two, three."

Now. Press the trigger. Aim for the eyes. Press the trigger. Too late. Too late. Had he pressed it? He opened his eyes. Again? He didn't see the eyes now.

That moan! He heard a long low moan and then a soul-splitting howl of terrible pain. What had he done? Were they death cries? Nothing was more dangerous than a wounded mountain lion. There she went again. He'd never heard anything more horrible in his whole life.

Neither had the horses. Several tried to make a break for it. They knew the cry of the wounded mountain lion. Martin sprang into action. He yelled and hooted and whipped them back into line with the strength of four men. Now he *had* to use the whip. Dimly he heard the others using their whips and hooting as he was. The thing to do was to get them back in a long thin line so that they couldn't terrify each other.

He yanked up colts and restored them to their mothers—separated two horses who had started to fight—dashed around others straying from the formation. Soon they had them back in line. The horses were really too tired to stampede.

But had he gotten the cat? Did they have a wounded puma trailing them? A wounded mountain lion would attack a man.

"Martin, are you all right? You got a clean shot. I think you killed her. Bravo!" Carlos yelled through the dust and confusion. Now he was slapping him on the back.

He noticed dimly that they were stopping. The herd was slowing gradually, an orderly slowing. That meant Epifanio would be along soon. What would he say? Would he be relieved, possibly pleased or—?

"You got her!" Alonso yelled from the rear.

"Huijaaaa!" Martin yelled. He'd done it. Then as suddenly as the exultation came, it was gone. So that was over. That danger was done. But would they ever reach the inn? He was so tired now he could die.

He looked up and saw the lights of the inn ahead. That meant they would be there in half an hour. Suppose the man wouldn't let them stay?

They had stopped. Some of the horses were lying down, calling it a night. Martin didn't blame them. Where was Epifanio?

"Congratulations! You'll have a fine skin to remember this night by," Carlos said.

"I do not need anything to remember this night by. Ever," Martin replied. "Where is Epifanio?"

"He and Alonso are tying the carcass to a horse so we can take it with us."

"Do we have to?" Martin asked.

"Have to what?"

"You know, take the carcass. Can't we just leave it?"

"Don't you want a puma rug for your floor?" Carlos was incredulous.

Martin shuddered. "It would have too many memories—of the night when I failed as well as tonight. Carlos, why don't you take the skin? I make you a present," Martin offered enthusiastically.

"You should give it to your uncle, Martin."

"If he wanted puma skins, he could have covered our house inside and out with the pumas he has killed," Martin answered proudly. His uncle must feel as he did.

"Thank you, *amigo*. I have always wanted one," Carlos said simply and with real gratitude. "Martin, do you see the lights? We are almost there," he added as if anxious to change the subject.

"*Bueno*, Martin. Well done!" Unexpectedly Epifanio was with him.

"Where did you come from?" The boys were both surprised.

"You are so tired you did not see me ride up?" his uncle asked.

"I feel numb. I should have gone to see if I got her after the shots, but I stayed to curb the horses. I did not know if I did right." Martin spoke like a small boy waking from a dream. At least he sounded to himself as if he did.

"Bravo! Segundo today but domador tomorrow!" Alonso shouted from his horse.

"You did *well*, segundo. It is always more important to care for the herd than the thief," Epifanio said firmly. "The cub will not bother us. Alone it will hunt jack rabbits."

Was any of it real? Martin was shaking all over. His uncle said he had done well and was shaking his hand. Carlos said they had the carcass tied to a horse. Tomorrow he would see it. He felt like throwing up, but it was very good to have Epifanio shaking his hand.

"Are you all right? Can you ride on to the inn now?" Epifanio sounded concerned.

"*Sí*, I can ride. What are we waiting for?" Martin answered with spirit.

"*Magnifico!* On to Condor Inn. We ride. *Vamos!*"

The long tired herd gradually got to its feet. The whips snapped, the horses whinnied and threw back their ears and tore at the rocky ground in a last desperate effort. They were on their way. They could see the lights ahead, and they were going to meet them.

Martin heard Epifanio give his cry, wild and exultant. He knew his uncle was proud of him. It was all right.

Chicken Hawk at
Condor Inn

MARTIN AND CARLOS RODE AT THE REAR AS THEY
climbed the last distance toward the flickering lights
of the inn. The herd seemed a staggering, battered
caravan to Martin, weaving shadows under the pale
light of the stars. He heard hoofbeats and the buzz of
crickets and the hooting of owls.

Before them was the dead puma, stiffening as it
hung across a pack horse's back, trailing blood over
the rocky trail. It would have to be skinned in the
morning or they'd have vultures for company by
afternoon. He hoped he did not have to skin the dead
cat. It was his job. But he wanted no part of it. Nor
did he want the skin. He had no pride in that kill
except that he'd been able to do what had to be done.

143

Let Carlos take the skin for a souvenir of the drive. He'd given the hide to Carlos. Maybe Carlos would do the skinning.

Martin felt better. Epifanio was pleased with him. He'd been no coward tonight. And they'd found Marta when there was no reason to hope they might. Martin searched the shadowy horses for one that was lighter and pulled slightly to the left, but she was just one of more than two hundred tonight. He could not make her out now. It was enough to know she was there!

She was back thanks to Epifanio, who rode stiff and proud at the very fore of the herd, as if he were leading an army.

Martin watched in surprise as Epifanio suddenly took off at full gallop, straight for the Condor Inn. What was going on? Martin edged over toward Carlos. Then he laughed aloud. Alonso was playing the gay Carnivalito on his harmonica.

> *Punta le mi*
> *Le va cantar*
> *Todos bailan,*
> *Todos cantan . . .*

The gay school song sounded incongruous. They had come through purgatory, and Alonso was playing folk dances!

"*Qué cosa*, Alonso, no?" He said to Carlos, surprised to hear his own voice.

"*Sí*, and what a character is your uncle too," Carlos answered.

"Maybe he has found another stray horse?"

"No, I think he's gone ahead to see if he can make arrangements for us so there won't be trouble," Carlos said.

"Trouble? You are always looking for trouble, you lawyers. The man at the hotel has to let us stay. It is the custom."

"It *was* the custom in Epifanio's day. But, if you were an innkeeper trying to maintain your hotel for presidents and royalty, would you welcome more than two hundred and twenty-five horses as non-paying guests?"

"They don't sleep in feather beds, and we pay for those we use!"

"They eat."

"So?"

"They also drink a great deal of water and they lose it. . . ."

"Epifanio wouldn't have planned to stop if we couldn't stay here," Martin said; but remembering Epifanio's doubtful "maybe," he wasn't so sure.

Carlos shrugged. They rode on in silence. No one would have the heart to turn them away. Martin was so tired the only thing that kept him going was the thought of those feather beds. And perhaps he would warm his hands before that great fire first. A steaming

bowl of stew would taste good. He could stay awake
long enough for that.

"How long now?" he asked Carlos.

"A few minutes. Our host is digesting our thunder
now, if he isn't too busy with Epifanio."

"Carlos, are we wrong to want to stay?"

"We have no choice. It would be suicide to try to
make the high pampa tonight. But for just this reason,
the man who owns this hotel must see every herd
that seeks the pampa. Suppose he is not a horse lover?"

"Well, you certainly don't sound upset by the
whole idea!"

"It might prove exciting."

"*Loco!*"

Martin slapped his whip against his saddle. He was
too tired to try to figure anything tonight. All he
wanted was to sleep one night in a feather bed. Was
this too much to ask?

There it was, the Condor Inn, dead ahead. It looked
like a castle made of wood and glass and hung in the
sky. It seemed even higher and larger than it had in
Doña Marta's book. It sparkled with warm yellow
lights. There were the broad wooden steps.

Epifanio stood on the long veranda with a man who
might have been his double. He was a gaucho, to
judge from his bombachas and boots and broad black
leather belt and the half moons carved on both
cheeks. The scars showed white under the lights. So
did those on Epifanio's face. They were face to face

and not very happy about the encounter, judging by their grim, straight mouths. Carlos had been right.

Alonso waved to them to slow the herd. The horses obeyed as if in their sleep. Horses and boys stayed and watched the men by the lights from the hotel.

"Water I'll give to any man or beast as long as I have it to give. Shelter is something we provide for people only. Ride them on to the high pampa. You've experience enough to dare." This was the innkeeper who spoke.

"I'll dare anything another man dares and more, and I have since the day I learned to walk. Your face shows you know well it's sure death for a herd to cross the divide by night. I told you about the storm we've already endured. We ask only six hours' shelter, and we'll pay for our board," Epifanio said evenly.

"How will you pay for an orchard ruined and trampled and eaten for fodder? I've nursed that orchard for twenty years."

"Many's the herd it's survived, then."

The other man snorted just once, but it told all.

"You must let us stay. It's the law of the land!"

"You're an old man to think that, Epifanio Guimenez!"

"Not too old to teach a needed lesson in hospitality."

With those words Epifanio jumped down from the veranda and opened a gate to his left, the gate to the pasture, and signaled the horses in. His opponent was there, quick as a flash, and kicked it back shut, pulling his knife as he did to make the action stick. His steel facón flashed level and sure in the pale light. Epifanio drew too with a smile on his face. They whipped off their ponchos as if they were twins, and wrapped them around their right arms for protection.

Epifanio shrugged as he leaped back to make room for the fight. He tried the edge of his knife on a clump of pampa grass and found it good. Neither wasted his breath on more words. What had to be done had to be done. This was the law of the pampa.

A nod from Epifanio told the boys that they must sit on their mounts and keep the herd still to await the issue. Death would not be the decider here, except in the case of an accident.

This was for honor and for fodder for horses, and the two could not be separated. Victory would be carved in a long half moon from temple to chin. If Epifanio carved well, then food and shelter was theirs with a smile. If he did not, then the other gaucho would carve, and they would leave without stopping for water. Now was the time to pray.

The men both backed off a bit, each hoping the other would close in first. There was as much danger in acting too fast as too slow in a fight with a knife. Each seemed willing to wait all night, though Epifanio gritted his teeth and the innkeeper snarled like a dog. Then the innkeeper trailed the end of his

poncho along the ground as they circled around, hoping to trip Epifanio, but that was too old a trick.

Epifanio laughed as he gave yet more ground to draw the other on, and the other whipped his poncho back around his arm where it might do more good. Both slipped their spurs then, to free their feet. This would be a good fight, for they both knew all the tricks in a gaucho's trade. And they tried the ground round about, scuffing for rocks and refuse that might trip a man when he had his mind on a fight.

The two knives gleamed by the light of the moon as they circled now, never one taking his eyes from the other even to wink. They'd been trained on the same pampa. If the first lunge missed the mark, the opponent got the next chance.

The innkeeper lunged! He missed but only by luck. Epifanio feinted and then drove for the face and left a mark but only a scratch. Not good enough.

Now came the chance for surprise. They waited again. Epifanio could wait as long as the next man. His opponent already bled. They circled again, each watching to see what the other would do. Quick and sly, as he sucked in his lips, the man from the Condor Inn found Epifanio's face as he lunged. Blood spurted. It was a piece of ear. The cheeks were not marked.

Now they fought! You could hear the knives scrape in the night. There was the sound of scuffling feet and breathing that was heavy and hot. How many times did they try and how many times find a mark? No one knew.

But neither flinched and neither was willing to quit, though both gushed blood. The half moon from eyelid to chin was missing yet. The outcome was not decided.

They circled once more, and knives flashed in the night. Both were grunting now and looking for any opening. Epifanio stood quiet a moment, watching as the other danced from side to side, jabbing when he might and retreating as quick as he jabbed. Suddenly, both lunged at once and they grappled then, hand to hand, each forcing the face of the other with the blade of a steel facón.

"Ugh!" "Ow!" Both yelled as they unexpectedly drew apart and threw their knives to the ground. Someone must be marked. It was over. Knives gleamed along in the dirt. Who was the winner?

"A fair fight?" Epifanio asked of the other man.

"A fair fight. Your ear is hurt. A pity," the gaucho replied.

The boys jumped from their horses.

"I think my cut is not deep," the man went slyly on. "I'll likely have no scar at all." They all pressed in to see, ignoring Epifanio's ear, for the winner was still in doubt. The man with the least wound was the winner here. What he said was true enough. The half moon was clear and well placed but just of the flesh.

"Just a tip off my ear. A nothing. Fleas have done

152

more," Epifanio said as blood gushed from his ear. He was right, the tip was gone forever to remind him of this night at the inn. Martin ripped up a shirt and offered half to each to sop up the blood while they decided what to do next. Horses slept where they stood. Men and boys said not a word for a moment.

Epifanio pushed out his free hand, and the gaucho shook it hard. They were friends. But the question remained. Neither had really won. Each was waiting for the other to speak, to give ground, but this was a game both knew. They might stand there all night.

Martin guessed Epifanio would never give ground if they stood there a week. The devil himself couldn't be quieter when he had something to gain. Martin also knew better than to offer help. He just hoped the shirt was enough to stanch the blood from the ear. Epifanio's hope was to belittle that wound.

The inkeeper scratched his left leg, picked up his knife, wiped it again and again, and finally stuck it slowly into his belt. He was getting nervous. Finally he sighed and he spoke.

"*Muy bien!* I've never been short when it comes to a stranger at the door. It's been a while since I've had a good talk. And that ear needs attention. You may stay one night, you and your nags. But only outside of the gates where your horses will not eat grass I planted for lawn or ruin my poor trees."

"I accept and with many thanks. Even the pasture outside the gate is better than they've had for a while.

It's better to let a hen take a chance than kill it to cure the pip, as the saying goes. And water?"

"Didn't they get enough water in the storm? Yes, Water too, if you must. But you have to be gone tomorrow, before the sun rises. There's a hunting party coming, a bus load and more."

"I give you my word," Epifanio said.

So it was settled. They would sleep under quilts in feather beds after all, once they'd bound up two men's wounds.

"Lindorfo Dominquez, at your service." The innkeeper bowed to the boys and then shook Epifanio's hand once again. "My home is your home," he continued, using the old salute.

The Condor's Nest

"Lindorfo certainly looked pleased when we left. Didn't he think we'd leave before his hunters arrived?" Martin asked Carlos as they struggled up the last steep and rocky path to the mountain pampa the next morning.

"He *did* look worried when we accepted his gracious invitation to breakfast! But I think he was delighted with the manure our horses left for his precious orchard. I can see him out there shoveling now," Carlos laughed.

"If he'd let us stay in the pasture, he wouldn't have had to shovel. And he wouldn't have a gash down the side of his face either."

"Which reminds me, how is Epifanio's ear?"

154

"He says it doesn't bother him as much as the flea bite on his arm."

"I'll bet! Well, he met his equal in Lindorfo's wife. It was just as if she never noticed the fight or the gash in her husband's face or the horses. I'll bet she's served a lot of stew to Lindorfo's knifing companions." Carlos swung out his whip to bring a stray colt back into the line. The path was rocky, and horses slipped out of place easily. There was a frisky air about the herd this morning.

And not only the herd. Carlos kept twisting his head around as if it were on a swivel.

"What's wrong with you? You're nervous as a cat," Martin said.

"Oh, I just hoped we'd see a condor. I've never seen one except in the zoo. Wouldn't you like to see a condor take off from a cliff and fly, Martin? Wouldn't you?" Carlos flapped his arms and nearly fell off his horse.

"Maybe you'd better leave flying to the condors," Martin suggested. "Epifanio said they used to live near where the hotel is, but not many came back after the hotel was built. He says we're more likely to see them up on the pampa itself."

"And here we are!" The herd was pulling to a halt. Martin and Carlos rode forward to join Epifanio and Alonso. They were on the very edge of the Pampa Achala, the highest plain in Argentina. Epifanio raised his arm to beckon them, and they sat gazing over the plain. No one said a word.

Before them the land stretched perfectly flat as far as they could see. There was not one tree, or hill, or fence, or even a house to break the sweep of the pampa grass. The grass moved in the wind like a tide, showing now all silver underleaves and again the gray green of the plant itself. A few small outcroppings of rock only strengthened the tide effect, as if they were foam riding the crosscurrents of an otherwise calm sea.

Even the strong wind blowing eternally across this wild land sounded muted. It blew in a low hypnotic hum. Martin could not take his eyes away.

"It is said that God himself visits the Pampa Achala," he murmured.

"And it is said that the devil speaks with him here," Carlos finished.

"I wonder what they discuss," Alonso said. "But looking at that grass, I'd say the worst of this drive was over. And we came through the hailstorm without pneumonia too!" He spoke happily to Epifanio, and they were all surprised to see the old gaucho cross himself.

"Do not tempt the fates. Anything can happen in three days. The worst is not over until the drive itself is over and the horses are safe in Calamuchita; and even then they may all die of disease they got on the way or be hit by hailstones and die of pneumonia next year. " Epifanio clucked his tongue and waved his finger in front of Alonso's nose.

"Only a fool counts his sheep before the slaughter," the gaucho went on. "Many years ago I was such a fool on this very pampa. I was almost as young as Carlos here and had worked a man's day on the ranches for more than two years. That year the drought was hard and the grass scarce, so the gauchos on the ranches nearby brought their herds up to the high pampa for a week or two weeks—enough to fatten them so they'd survive the dry year. Then they'd return to their ranches so as not to take more than their share.

"Well, to make a long story short, one herd came and stayed on and on until the gauchos thought they had papers on the land; they began to object if anyone else came on with a few starving steers. This was all their own private property to hear them say it out.

"We were unhappy with the cutthroats running this herd. We brought our herds from time to time and bore many a grudge with a turn of the cheek until finally one night they went too far. So the very next night we made out we were turning back and at midnight returned to have it out by the knife. There were about fifty of us."

"How many of them were there?"

"That was the surprise. We thought there were just about twenty. You can imagine our surprise when we arrived and saw that they had us two to one, and the night on their side. For to storm a camp already dug in by night is all right if you come by stealth, but they were armed and waiting for us, hand on their knives."

"Someone like Lindorfo must have told."

"No, it was in the wind. But Lindorfo was there, an apprentice like me; he told me last night. We waited the night out, though it was little sleep we had, and we attacked with the dawn.

"The fight was to kill. Not on our side at first, but they killed one of our men and then another, and two is no accident. After the second death, we gave no quarter.

"We fought all the morning, with the cattle milling and lowing among us. You would think they'd have gotten out of the way with the first wild yell, but they had to be right in the thick of it.

"My hand ached from clutching the knife. I had blood spurting out from all over me like juice from an orange, but it was my first fight and I was enjoying it. Riderless horses neighed for their masters and you rode over dead bodies as often as not. To this day I wonder the cattle didn't stampede and kill every one of us fools. They held, though, and it began to look as if there would be no victory that day for one side or the other.

"It finally got to a pass where you couldn't be sure who was on which side, what with the blood and the wind and the dust. But a man couldn't turn tail and run, even if the moaning was beginning to wear through to the marrow of your bone and you were afraid of killing a friend by mistake.

"Well, we might have been fighting there yet if it were not for this pampa, itself. One minute it was clear and blue as this sky, and the next—you might not believe me and I cannot blame you for that—but the next minute we were having a blizzard. Not any old storm that might come in the fall of the year, but a blizzard with snow and sleet and the wind blowing a gale.

"Then we had to get the wounded off the pampa or they and we and every man alive would have ended his days right there. It made no difference if the wounded were friends or foes. It was haul over the edge of the pampa where the sky was still blue and the day still warm.

"I only tell you this tale to show that you can't count on a thing in this life. Least of all on this prairie that is like no other in all the world. The worst is never over," Epifanio predicted dourly, and then went on. "As I think of this pampa perhaps it is best if we camp right here on the edge where we've got the bluffs behind us and can scoot over the edge if we have to. Though I'm not expecting snow today," he added, smiling and waving toward the mountains, which rose behind them and formed a backdrop to the pampa.

"I wonder if we can trust even the *weathervane* in this place," Carlos teased.

Martin and Alonso did not speak. Instead they stared at Epifanio. Had he really been in that battle? For everyone had heard of the Battle of Pampa Achala that ended in a freak snowstorm.

"But what *was* the final insult that led up to the fighting that day, the day of the snowstorm?" Martin asked.

"I was just a boy and was never told," Epifanio answered quietly. He seemed puzzled about the question for the first time.

Martin looked at his uncle in wonder. He was just like the pampa. Proud, inspiring, and impetuous. Here he had almost lost his life in a battle, and he had never known why he fought!

Epifanio gave them no more time to ponder his tale or the wide pampa but sent them right to their chores. There was work to be done and water to find before the wind came on strong, by mid-afternoon at the latest. Carlos scouted enough wood to keep a fire going twenty-four hours. Alonso saw to the horses. Martin stowed the food and other gear in a niche in the cliff where it would be relatively safe from wind, sand, and stray animals.

Only when they were through and sitting down did Epifanio spread out his map. Each boy knew he must trace out the route again even though each thought he knew the way to Calamuchita by heart.

"Here's where we are, and I've marked what we have yet to cross in red pencil. Mark it well in case you get lost or separated by the wind or your own inclination." The boys laughed at the idea of anyone leaving the drive willingly.

They would have a good ten or twelve hours' ride across the mesa tomorrow. It shouldn't be bad if the wind was with them. Then they would dip down into Copina Valley and spend the night. There should be both fodder and water there. Epifanio had word that the river was running. It was a steep canyon, but only half a day's ride beyond was Bosque Alegre, which Doña Marta called a clump of trees. From there it would be a day and a half into Calamuchita. Martin looked up, satisfied that he understood.

"All right? Now, one or two trifles to keep in mind. It's been ten years and more since I scouted that valley; but as I remember, it had beauty, snakes, and a steep cliff. Reminded me of the Garden of Eden, except that it was harder to leave. The trail was steep and furnished with enough loose rocks to send a foolish horse plunging. Once over the top it's only a couple of hours to Bosque Alegre. Three or four at the most."

"But where do we meet my father?" Alonso asked.

"And why do they call it Bosque Alegre, the happy forest, when it's no more than a clump of trees?"

"And why do we stop there at all when it's not a full day's trip?" Carlos asked.

"Ah, not to stop would be robbing Don Jaime of the pleasure of riding on down with us. He says that he plans to meet us a few miles south of the bosque. *Bueno?* We must let him know. All right. Who wants to ride after water? According to Lindorfo we'll get nothing for our search."

Martin thought that his uncle would find water if only to prove Lindorfo wrong. He hoped he didn't have to go. He wanted some time by himself.

"I'll race my gray against one of your blacks," Alonso challenged. Alonso was proud of his mount and rightly so. He'd been waiting for this chance. They all looked to Epifanio to see if he'd take up the challenge.

"Hyyyyaaaiiii!" he shouted, leaping to his horse. "But look for water as you eat my dust," Epifanio called back as he rode off.

Alonso rode off after him at a full gallop, and soon they were two specks on the horizon.

"May the best horse win," Carlos said, waving his hat in the air.

"They could pass a lake and not know there was water, at that pace," Martin added.

"Alonso isn't the only one who feels the worst is over," Carlos said, indicating the horses. There *was* a gaiety about them today, and it must be good to frolic in tall grass after climbing over rocks for seven days. Perhaps they felt this was like their own mountain pasture in Chepes—only lusher. Here, when a horse finished eating he lay down and wallowed in the luxurious grass. The sun shone on their coats, making them look sleeker than they were. Flattering sun. They were a gaunt and ribby herd compared to the sleek and proud Arabians they had been six months before.

Martin warmed his hands by the small fire as Carlos prepared maté. The horses were content, the herb tea smelled wonderful, and there was nothing he had to do. Carlos was planning to read, but Martin intended to sit by the fire.

Suddenly the sky grew dark. He looked up through the shadow and saw an enormous black bird glide through the sky over them and over the entire herd without once using his wings. It swooped not only over them but caught another air current and carried itself back to the cliff with one wing flap.

The condor! That could only be the condor! They both knew it and knew they would never again see anything quite so graceful. So each held his breath, and neither said anything.

High on the bluff directly above them perched the bird they had watched and another, probably his mate. Martin thought he saw still another smaller bird behind them. The condor lifted his wings to fly again, hunching them high and then spreading them wide as he glided off the bluff. He flew without effort, riding the air currents.

Instinctively Martin raised his own arms and then dropped them. "It is a foolish sheep who thinks himself a wolf and sets out to find his brothers," he said

repeating the old proverb.

"It would almost be worth it," Carlos said gently. "But you should see one of them try to get off the ground at the zoo. Its body is so heavy it takes half an hour or more of flapping and screeching."

The condor might have awkward moments on alien ground; but on the pampa, in his native land he was king. Martin watched the two great birds sitting still as if movement were the furthest thing from their minds. Their bodies were dark brown with a white *T* under the breast. Even their bald orange heads and hooked beaks were perfectly still. Only the beady eyes moved, forever searching, the eyes of a bird of prey. But bird of prey or no, the condor was always a bird to respect. Unlike hawks or common vultures, the condor never attacked an animal until the creature was dead.

Now the two birds seemed to be nudging something toward the edge of the cliff. An animal of some sort.

"It's a baby!" Carlos whispered.

"They're going to push it off. They can't!"

"No!"

The bird gave one loud piercing screech before it went over the edge. It plummeted at first, but like a man with a parachute, its wings suddenly went out and it started flapping madly. It was a baby condor, trying desperately to stay aloft. Once they saw that the baby would try, both of the elder condors swooped easily down and glided along with it, urging him toward air currents.

"But suppose he didn't make it?"

"You learned to walk, didn't you?"

"Yes, but I could fall down and start all over again."

"I read that baby condors stay in the nest a whole year. After nursing that baby a year, the mother wouldn't just let him fall."

"She pushed him out."

"What I want to see is how he gets back up to the nest."

The baby was getting the feel of it now, trusting himself to glide a while and feeling his strong wings able to bear him along. Then he lost confidence and flapped furiously before one parent managed to guide him back to an updraft.

"I never had anyone help me," Martin thought jealously. He wondered if Epifanio had helped him learn to walk. He must have. He had probably treated him like a colt. The baby condor was lucky to have a mother and father, even if they did push him out of the nest.

The baby caught an updraft that landed him right on the ledge. Martin saw him draw back away from the edge. His parents allowed him to rest, but within a few minutes the baby himself edged toward the point and took off into the sky by himself. He did this several times during the afternoon until the wind

grew so strong that it buffeted him in different directions. Then the entire condor family retired back into their nest somewhere up in the cliffs.

"I guess that's all," Carlos sighed.

"I'm glad only you and I were here," Martin said shyly.

"It seems almost as if we were alone with the condors."

"I know. Let's keep it a secret," Martin said sud-

denly. He and Carlos had once had all kinds of
secrets. They shook hands on it.

It was late afternoon before they saw dust balls
that must be Epifanio and Alonso riding over the
horizon. Now that the condors had surrendered the
sky, it was filled with all kinds of birds taking their
last frenzied flights of the day. They looked fussy
after the gliding giants. Busy and tiny, like so many
bees.

Epifanio and Alonso rode up with a flourish. They looked wind-blown and excited.

"No water, but we met a gaucho who says there is plenty in Copina Canyon," Alonso explained.

"Who won?"

Alonso and Epifanio laughed together, and the boys could not get them to say more.

"What did you do all afternoon? You weren't busy with supper, I see."

"Oh, nothing. Just sat," Martin replied with a wink at Carlos.

The Valley of Death

It had been a grim race over the wind-blasted pampa, but now they were down in the quiet valley. It was well after dark as they maneuvered the final distance down the steep wall of the canyon onto the floor of the valley, single file. They were too tired to do more than sense that they had found a haven. They slept, and only by daylight saw an oasis well worth every treacherous step. The valley was soft and green and gay with bright flowers. More than a year had passed since any of them had seen growth as lush as this. The air, too, was balmy as a spring morning. And for the first time on the drive, the famished horses had all the feed and water they wanted.

The four herdsmen spent a long time over breakfast that morning, relishing the fresh milk and warm bread bought from a tiny store on the very edge of the pampa before they plunged over. They heaved a sigh of relief over their second cup of coffee. It was good to sit, comfortable and companionable. Especially, Martin thought, when in another two and a half days the drive would be over. He and Carlos would be getting haircuts and sensible clothes for school. Another three weeks and they would be studying history instead of making it, and there seemed to be no comparison between the two.

"Perhaps they will have an asado in our honor when we ride into Calamuchita," Alonso said eagerly.

"Eh?" Epifanio snorted. "A man can't do a week's work without having the fatted calf killed in his honor?"

"Oh, the day of the gaucho is over," Carlos chanted. Epifanio only smiled. Martin marveled again that Carlos could get away with so much. His uncle would be furious with him or anyone else on the ranch for that remark. But then Epifanio seemed to have mellowed the last few days.

"Alonso, your father may not be overjoyed when we come in twelve horses short," Epifanio continued. This was true, and the thought quieted the boys.

"And has it rained yet over the valley of Chepes?" Alonso asked in return, implying that the horses were better off with them than at home.

Martin said nothing. Something was nagging at

him. He had an odd feeling that there was a problem somewhere. The horses had everything they could want, and yet they were strangely restless this morning. He hunted for Marta with his eyes, to see how she was feeling, as a guide to the others, but could not find her. What was wrong? Was it just his restless imagination? "Horses did a lot of whinnying last night," he said tentatively.

"Just too much of a good thing—water and fodder all in the same day," Carlos answered comfortably.

But Epifanio gave Martin a strange look, as if the same feelings had been bothering him; and he leaped to his feet and ran down to the herd.

"You're right. Let's see," he called back. Martin's feet felt like lead as he followed. Alonso's face turned white. Martin knew he was thinking of the superstition he'd ignored yesterday. The horses looked all right. Perhaps they were just restless.

"That gray lying in the water—on her side—the speckled mare," Alonso said fiercely. Martin's eyes followed to where Alonso pointed. A great gray mare lay clumsily on her side in the middle of the creek. The other horses gave her a wide berth. And no wonder.

Martin gasped.

"Sí, she must be dead," Alonso said with certainty. Epifanio reached her first, splashing wildly through the water.

"She's already swelling. Dead several hours," he

said. "*Chicos, vamos,* see about the others. And be careful, eh?"

The old gaucho pulled off his boots and knelt with the horse in the water, his wide bombachas legs billowing unheeded while he checked over every inch of the carcass. Satisfied, he beckoned to Carlos, who still stood nearby, and pointed out two small blue marks a quarter of an inch apart on the horse's neck.

"Fang marks?" Carlos asked, jumping involuntarily.

"*Sí.* The víbora de la cruz, I think. I'd like a peso for each one I've killed in these hills. Struck on the neck while she slept so the poor devil never had a chance. We couldn't have helped if we'd seen it done. When he strikes on the leg there's sometimes a chance but—well, there's nothing to do now but haul the body out and hope we haven't already contaminated the water supply.

Carlos was afraid to touch the swelling rigid leg Epifanio pointed out to him, but he was even more afraid of the look in the old gaucho's eye. So, gritting his teeth and trying to stop his nose against the smell, he took a leg and pulled. Nothing happened. Even when they both pulled in unison they were lucky to gain an inch at a try. But one way or another they had finally hauled the carcass up on the mossy bank and were turning away to take their first deep breath when Martin screamed.

"Martin! Are you bitten?"

"Martin, where are you?"

Epifanio and Carlos shoved their way through the milling horses to see Martin sprawled on the grass beside Marta. She was breathing in great gulps. Epifanio knelt and quickly found the telltale fang marks on her right foreleg, just above the hoof.

"Again," Epifanio said, and no one knew if he meant that Marta was again in trouble or that another horse had been bitten. He pointed out the marks and asked Martin, "And you?"

"Fine. But she wasn't making a sound. Just lying here, and when I came over she tried to nuzzle me."

"Good. Martin, Carlos, hold her!"

As he spoke, Epifanio pulled out his knife and burned the blade with a match. "Hold her," he whispered again, and plunged the knife into her leg. He cut a cross where the fangs had been, while the horse neighed piteously. The boys held her fast. Epifanio bent down, put his mouth to the cross cut and sucked out the blood himself. He spat it out on the ground. Three times he did this, each time covering the blood with dirt and grass so no other horse would take the poison by accident.

"*Basta*, all over," he said, and the boys released the mare who kicked to be sure she was free and then lay still, breathing irregularly. She kept frightened eyes on Martin.

"What do they look like, these víbroas de la cruz?" asked Martin through clinched teeth.

"Aren't you afraid of swallowing some poison?"

Carlos asked. Carlos kept looking around as if he were searching for something or someone.

"I've sucked a snake's poison a hundred times and more but never without asking God's help," Epifanio said seriously. "Martin, when you think how easily a snake is killed by a hoof, you have to admit there's no use blaming them if they bite to protect themselves. As to the appearance of these, they're devils to see since they're not much over a foot long and the color of mud. You'll know them by the white cross on their head. This is the worst time of year because their nests are full of young." As he talked, Epifanio was poulticing the leg with mud. He seemed to be talking as much to Marta as to the boys. Finally he asked Martin to continue. "You can do this until Alonso gets back with the herbs; I'd better check over the rest of the herd."

"Oh!"

Martin and Epifanio turned to Carlos. He looked as if he were going to faint.

"What's wrong? Are you all right?"

"*Sí*, but I saw Alonso ride off like the devil himself were after him, and—well—I was afraid—"

"Afraid of what"

"That he might think the devil *was* after him," Carlos answered simply. None of them *really* believed in supersition, but Martin knew that if he were Alonso he would feel uneasy this morning after predicting that the worst was over yesterday. Still there was no need for Carlos to worry.

"Hey, you don't believe in superstitions, not a lawyer," Martin said, looking to his taciturn uncle for help. Carlos was also watching Epifanio, whose face told nothing. He seemed to be scanning the horses.

"No, I don't. But my brother and Epifanio sometimes think differently. They belong to the pampas and the traditions of the past. Why do you think Doña Marta chose Alonso instead of me to teach all about herb medicines?"

"Carlos, I am a gaucho," said Epifanio, finally. "I only worry about what I see and know I can help. Now, I know we must stop chattering like hens and help these horses. They are not even gauchos, but only horses, and so we can help them a little."

"*Gracias*. Shall I bring some salve?" Carlos looked relieved. Martin wondered again at the understanding there seemed to be between his uncle and his best friend. Epifanio even understood Carlos wanting to be a lawyer, which was more than Martin could. Marta writhed, and Martin gently patted more mud on her leg.

Martin watched Epifanio and Carlos move through the herd carefully, spreading salve on all old wounds as they examined each animal for two small marks. The horses were so used to treatment now that they hardly noticed.

"Three bitten. We found a black stallion in a bad

way. *Sí*, bitten on the leg. Drought has driven the snakes as well as our horses to this wet valley," Epifanio said when they finally returned.

"The valley of death," Martin said bitterly. "I thought snakes crawled under rocks and kept warm during the night."

Epifanio shrugged. "Last night was warm."

"Don't you hate them too?"

"No, but I would kill any I saw."

"Alonso shouldn't be out alone in a country crawling with snakes," Carlos said.

"I think I hear hoofbeats now," Epifanio said, holding up a hand for silence. How could he hear anything over the noise of the herd?

But in a few minutes Alonso came riding into camp. There was a great sheaf of weeds tied to the back of his saddle.

"You shouldn't have been out alone," Carlos muttered, but Alonso paid no attention. He and Epifanio were going over the weeds, rubbing them between their palms until they had a mixture like tea leaves. Then Epifanio took boiling water from the fire and poured it over the herbs in a pot, making a strong tea. When the tea cooled, they brushed away the drying mud at the snake bites and poured the liquid on the wounds. Neither horse objected. Marta even sucked a little tea when Alonso held the pan to her mouth. The stallion clenched his teeth, and they had to stop bothering him.

"More mud," Epifanio told Martin. He ran between the two horses, who were five hundred feet apart, slapping mud on each, wondering what would happen next. Epifanio couldn't risk keeping the whole herd in the valley until the two horses either died or got well. But both would surely die without care. Still, Epifanio must do what was right for the whole herd.

"Well?" Alonso asked Epifanio.

"*Vamos*. We must leave before the sun warms this valley of death and wakes more of its tenants," he said looking at Martin.

"What about Marta and the stallion?" Carlos asked. Martin could have hugged him for asking first.

"True. We have already lost thirteen."

"I'll stay. Could I, please?" Martin begged, blushing at his weakness.

"On the other hand, we cannot ride well with only three men, and we would leave you in a valley of frightened snakes." Suddenly Epifanio snapped his fingers. He smiled.

"With your permission?" Martin asked again.

"Stay today if you wish, Martin. We can make it to Bosque Alegre without you and will wait there. I will send a gaucho I know back here to watch them, if they live, until they are able to move. When he relieves you, can you find the bosque? Good. We will wait until sunrise."

"You'll send someone from the ranch?"

"No, I have an old friend who lives just over the canyon. He knows this snake and its bite well and will know what can be done. Now listen. Keep your gun with you at all times. Shoot any snake you see. Here is extra ammunition. If one of the horses goes berserk, you will have to shoot it. Understand? That is an order. It might kill others and its calls bring the wild animals if you do not. Keep the fire going and give them the herb tea once an hour. Keep the poultices wet. Give them water. We will leave what ponchos we can to keep them warm. Any questions?"

"What should I do if they die?" Martin asked steadily.

The three turned in surprise at Martin's words, sensible though they were. What should he do with three carcasses, one of a well-loved horse?

Epifanio nodded approvingly at his nephew. "To be honest, we both know there's nothing to do but ride out of the valley, and the quicker the better," he said.

Martin nodded. He kept any other plans he might have to himself. "Don't forget to leave the ponchos. *Hasta la vista*. Oh, matches?"

Epifanio threw him a pack of matches. Then he clapped his hands. Martin poulticed the horses as the other three broke camp. They moved quickly. Each knew his duties after a week of the same routine, and no one wasted a minute—though everyone looked carefully before placing his foot on new ground and jumped when a breeze blew the grass. Three horses were already bitten by snakes. They were probably waking all over the valley now, slithering through the green grass in search of a bug or a warm spot in the sun. One might be underfoot or behind a rock or even inside a warm saddlebag.

Martin was glad he had to poultice the horses, though it meant running the length of the camp from one to the other. He was glad because if he had to talk with Carlos or Epifanio they would soon see that he was not so sensible as his calm questions indicated. If they knew that he felt like jelly, they might not trust the two sick horses to him. They might be afraid he would go to pieces as he had that first night when he met the puma. He was afraid he might, terribly afraid.

Marta felt wet beneath his hand. Was sweating like this brought on by the herb tea or was it a sign of approaching death? Martin did not know. He had seen horses sweat when they reached the crisis in pneumonia and then recover.

Martin took off his poncho and rubbed Marta, trying to dry her off. Her breathing seemed even now, much better than the rasping of the black stallion. If only Epifanio got the poison before it ran through her blood stream. If only he himself had come out and checked the horses last night when they kept whinnying. Didn't Epifanio always say the lazy were worse than the bad?

"Martin!" His uncle stood over him looking as if he'd called his name a number of times.

"Ready? Are you going now? Tell me the symptoms. When will I know? What more can I do for them?"

"*Bueno*. You see the symptoms—sweating, irregular breathing. I've also seen paralysis that men took for rigor mortis, and the dangerous business of going berserk. The venom works in a hurry; so if they live through the afternoon, the chances are good. Keep them cool enough now and warm when the wind comes up this afternoon. And keep an eye out yourself for the *víbora de la cruz*! If you are bitten, cut it and then wait for my friend. Good luck," said Epifanio, swinging astride his horse. He turned abruptly back to the herd.

Alonso shook hands next and left something cold and hard in Martin's hand. Another gun? No, it was the harmonica. Martin knew Alonso felt responsible for their trouble today, and he searched for a way to tell him superstitions were not important, but Alonso had turned away and was lost in the herd.

"*Gracias, gracias!*" he yelled, but Alonso was slapping his whip to the air and yelling to rouse the horses.

"*Amigo*. Catch!" Carlos threw down something, and Martin caught it. A lucky catch too, for it was his watch he tossed. "It might be good for something. *Adiós*."

"Carlos—" He had been about to say, "you are my best friend," which would have been ridiculous. Men didn't say such things; Martin was grateful for his narrow escape.

Marta tried to raise herself to follow the herd, and Martin had to hold her down, soothe her, and tell her they'd be joining the others later. He heard Gatito whinny from the tree he was tied to for safe-keeping. Even the wounded stallion got to his knees but could go no further and flopped to the ground with a thud that sounded through the valley. He snorted and coughed and cried in a shrill high whinny as the horses stepped carefully around them and wound up the steep canyon. Only when they were safely off the valley floor did Epifanio and the boys start their wild yells to urge the herd on faster, to force them up the rocky ravine.

Martin could hardly hear above the racket and thunder and dust of the herd moving out. They were balky this morning. There'd been water and grass here, and ahead there lay only a dry, steep ravine. They shook their manes and flashed their high tails and pawed the dust. But they moved. The sunlight caught flexing knees and flashing hoofs. Martin watched them work their way up the hillside, dodging falling rocks and outcroppings and bushes. He watched with pride and a sense of desolation. There was no better herd in all Argentina!

"See you at the Bosque Alegre," he called aloud.

It was the logical point for them to meet. Doña Marta's geography called it a clump of trees that rose suddenly in the midst of a wild, flat pampa, the only oasis in a desert of sand, rock, and mesquite. From there, they had only a day and a half ride down into the valley of Calamuchita—one day really, if the patrón were not going to join them. What more lay ahead before they reached Calamuchita? Martin couldn't even try to guess. He waited now until the dust settled so he could check the black stallion. In fifteen minutes time the horses were only shadowy forms picking their way against the ridge. The valley was quiet.

And he was alone with two snake-bitten horses and Gatito. Poor Gatito was tied to a tree at the opposite end of the valley. Epifanio said he should not be tied too near the sick horses or they might bite or kick him. He was grazing peacefully. Martin thought it would be better if he consolidated the camp a little, but he did not know how to go about it. He and Marta were about five hundred feet from the black stallion, who was in turn at least that distance from Gatito. This meant a lot of walking and not much companionship, but there seemed little he could do about it.

He ran to the creek and offered water in a tin plate to each horse. The black refused any, so Martin rubbed his lips and face with a damp cloth. He was lying in the sun and there seemed no way to shade him. Finally Martin rigged a poncho for a tent and this seemed to give him some relief, although his breathing was still so uneven it seemed ready to stop at any moment.

Marta actually sucked a little of the water. Did that mean she felt better than the stallion or only that, knowing Martin, she wished to please him. Both horses seemed drowsy now—or were they dying? No, because Gatito was sleeping too. Fortunately Gatito was sleeping standing up. He was much less likely to get bitten that way. Still Martin scanned the ground around him warily. If the sick horses died, he would be all alone in the world except for his faithful Gatito.

He looked at the sky and found with relief that there were no vultures yet, although the dead horse offered them food for the asking, and vultures were known to have picked out an animal's eyes even before he was dead.

He looked over the valley. A stream lined with weeping willow trees curved through the center. On either side lay small green meadows with outcroppings of rock and an occasional bush. Mountains rose rapidly on every side. Martin didn't see a sign of a snake in the dappled sunshine. But what had Epifanio said? You had the devil's own time seeing them because they were the color of mud.

Gradually as Martin continued scanning, he thought he saw something moving in the grass. When he looked closely, he could see slithering movements in several places. The grass was alive with—something —snakes? It must be. Snakes crawling all around him, great overgrown worms with white crosses crawling toward him. "No. No!"

Marta snorted and tried to get up. Martin realized he'd yelled aloud. What was wrong with him? He didn't see anything except grass and flowers out there. He was soaking with perspiration, and his hands felt clammy. He'd have to get hold of himself. He couldn't expect help much before sundown, which must be eight hours or more away.

Do something! First, get fresh mud for the horses. Offer them water. Poor Gatito who had to stay tethered to a tree all day—get him some water. Gather wood for a fire. Brew more herb tea. Where were those ground herbs? There was plenty to keep him busy if he did all the chores that were there to do. It might help if he whistled.

Sometime during the long afternoon the black stallion died. Martin was never sure when. He had gotten so that he poulticed and offered water and tea automatically, and if the horse did not drink he hardly noticed. He was slapping mud on the stallion's leg when he realized that it was stiff, and that he really knew the animal was dead because the flies were thicker there than around Marta or Gatito. Flies covered the swelling gray mare and had been bothering the sick horses all afternoon.

Martin ran back to Marta. She might have died too,

and he not have known. But she was breathing more normally than before. Two dead carcasses. Surely the vultures would be swooping down soon. And tonight the wild animals would come for their share. But he wouldn't be here tonight. Epifanio's gaucho friend would come by then, and he would know what to do.

Martin felt something hard and cold in his pocket. Alonso's harmonica. Gratefully he pulled it out, wiped it across his knee, and started to pick out a tune.

"I've never played this before, so you'll have to be patient," he told Marta. "But Epifanio tells me I whistle well." A slow tango seemed to soothe Marta. She lay quietly while Martin played the harmonica and shooed off the flies.

It began to grow dark while Martin played, and still the relief man did not come. Where was he? He had been lucky that no vultures had come, but the smell of the gray mare would bring carnivorous animals at night. The fire was out and he should build it up again. Marta would need a fire to keep her warm soon. A wind was coming up. Martin jabbed his knife savagely into the ground.

He had piled some firewood nearby, but not enough to last more than a couple of hours. He hadn't expected to need any. Where was that man? Epifanio was always trusting people. This was probably some old gaucho he'd known fifty years ago who took his money and laughed behind his back. He would probably never show up.

Regardless, Martin knew he had to get up and walk the hundred yards to Gatito and the saddlebags where matches and ponchos and food and his flashlight were. He must! It was dark now and impossible to tell where a snake might be; but without matches and the flashlight, he didn't have a chance in this wild country.

Martin got up and stuck the harmonica in his pocket. Gradually, resting at each step, and gingerly putting each foot down ever so slowly and gently, Martin inched his way toward the saddlebags. He was sure with each step that he felt the slimy body of a snake underfoot, and was relieved at each step to find it was only grass. Once he jumped, sure he'd gotten a snake. He threw his knife beside his foot. Got it. He was afraid to pull out his knife, afraid of the blood, or perhaps the snake was not really dead. He reached down and yanked at the knife. He had fatally stabbed a giant mushroom!

He called gently to Gatito, and the stallion answered uneasily. He called again. Gatito answered. Thank God! What would he do without him? Suppose Gatito was bitten? He'd never get out of here. The gray mare was somewhere around here. The stench was sickening. Martin gave the dead horse a wide berth though it meant many extra torturous steps.

Finally he reached the saddlebags and fumbled for the flashlight. He flashed it all around and took comfort at being able to see in the night. He leaned against Gatito for a few minutes, listening to his healthy regular breathing, and considered taking him over near Marta. They should all be together. Something might attack Gatito out here all by himself and away from the fire. He might get cold.

But Epifanio had said no. Gatito should stay away from the sick horses. He might get hurt. But wasn't it almost worse to leave him near a dead horse that might be attacked by a puma any minute? Martin moved Gatito to a tree farther from the mare and a little closer to the fire, and then reluctantly gathered the matches and flashlight and food and left him.

In a few minutes Martin had the fire going. It felt wonderful, and by its light he went to the river and put water on to boil. He'd make fresh herb tea and a cup of coffee for himself. Eating was out of the question because the stench of the dead animals hung over the whole valley now.

Still he felt better and wondered why he had been so frightened. After all, he had a gun in case of a wild animal, and he had Gatito. This was the same valley he had been in all day. As a matter of fact, the snakes were a lot less likely to bite in the night, and it was colder than last night had been, he thought, drawing his poncho close. Something must have delayed his relief, but he'd be along soon now and Martin would be with his uncle and Carlos and Alonso by morning.

All he had to do was take care of Marta and learn to play the harmonica. She did seem better.

"There's a girl. Epifanio said you'd have a good chance if you pulled through the afternoon, and he knows. So just take it easy. The worst is over. It's already after eight in the night by Carlos's watch, and your breathing is better than it was this afternoon." Martin didn't like the sound of his voice against the whistle of the wind in the trees. So he took out his harmonica and leaned against Marta for warmth. That way, too, he would know instantly if she needed him. She lay still, and might have been sleeping except that her eyes were open. Martin thought he saw her ears twitch forward as if she were listening to the tunes he picked out.

What was that? Martin broke off the gay carnival song he'd been playing and listened. He thought he heard twigs snap. It was hard to tell when the wind whistled as it did through this cavern. It sounded like the night of the storm. But no, it was a perfectly clear night. There it went again. A wild animal. Not a puma again! Martin felt cold sweat and goose pimples. A gun only helped if you saw the puma first. Otherwise—

But the horses weren't frightened. Gatito would be going wild if it were a puma, because he was tied up and helpless. He'd sense danger before Martin would. The fire was almost out.

Martin forced himself to leave Marta and go out

after more wood. He was afraid to go over by the saddlebags where the morning's fire had been. There was too much chance of meeting a snake or being far enough from the fire to make him easy prey for a wild animal. Instead he flashed his light on the ground nearby, and when he saw a large piece of wood, stepped gingerly toward it, trying to gather all the smaller pieces between him and the piece he particularly wanted in one trip. It became a game. How much wood could he find in how few steps? He was surprised to find it was nearly midnight by the time he was sure he had enough for the rest of the night.

Marta was sleeping peacefully. Her breathing seemed normal, and she wasn't sweating any more. Martin rubbed herb tea on her bite but no longer woke her to drink. She must be floating in herb tea by now. He huddled near her, hoping to keep them both a little warmer, hoping that some of his strength might flow over into her. He kept the fire up and played the harmonica to keep himself awake. He tried not to let himself look at Carlos's watch more than once every half hour. What difference did it make? When morning came, it would get light, and not before.

And as soon as it got light, no later, he must ride out of this valley and leave Marta to almost certain death. Though he felt the mare could live now, that she had passed the crisis, he knew he could not stay long enough to help her regain even enough strength to feed herself. Epifanio would be waiting for him. They needed a fourth man to take the horses across the wide stretch of pampa between Bosque Alegre and the place where Don Jaime would meet them. The herd would stray if it wasn't boxed in. They might lose two dozen horses; and Martin knew that he must go, not only because Epifanio expected him, but because the herd needed him. Perhaps he could return for Marta in a few days, but if she hadn't starved by then, the chances were wild animals or vultures would have found her. Especially with the dead horses nearby.

He no longer expected the other man to come. The brave gaucho had taken Epifanio's money and stuck it into the big pockets of his bombachas and thought *that* a good day's work. Martin stroked the sleeping horse sorrowfully and decided that at least he would leave water and fodder enough for several days. There just might be a chance. The night wore slowly on.

What was that? Just before dawn Martin thought he heard something come crashing through the underbrush. He cocked his gun. No wild animal would make that much noise.

"Stop or I'll shoot," he yelled.

"*Amigo*, do not shoot. "I come to help you," said a quiet voice from the underbrush. "Your uncle sent me to relieve you."

"Now?" Martin asked.

"The delay was not mine, but God's," the voice

explained gently. "My youngest son broke a leg and I had to ride all night to the doctor, but I came as soon as I could."

The man rode into the clearing, and Martin could see that he was drenched in sweat, and his exhaustion also supported his story. He was a man well into his forties and looked as if he had spent rugged days under the stars and the sun. He was a gaucho.

Martin put away his gun. "I am very glad to see you," he said.

"You must hurry or you will miss your rendezvous with Epifanio, eh?" The man dismounted as he spoke and bent down to examine Marta. He put his hand first to her chest, nodded, and then ran it lightly along her body. He examined her eyes and mouth. Martin brought her water and she lapped it greedily.

"Good," the man said. "And the other?"

"Dead."

"Well, this mare owes you her life. I would wish my own son might do so well."

"Thank you," Martin whispered.

"Now you must ride like the wind, *amigo*."

Martin wished Marta *hasta la vista*, commended her to the stranger's care, and mounted Gatito.

He could hardly believe that the night was over and he was riding out of the valley of death.

Race for Green Pastures

"HUIJAAAA! SHOW YOUR RUMP TO THE WIND!" MAR-
tin urged Gatito on and on over the dry, rocky pampa
toward the Bosque Alegre. Would he reach the forest
before his uncle had to leave with the herd? They'd
lose more horses if he weren't there to form one side
of Epifanio's box for the herd. He judged it had been
a good three hours since sunrise, but he saw the forest
now. Eight-thirty by Carlos's watch. They couldn't
wait much longer and meet Don Jaime as they'd
planned.

"Gallop, Gatito! Show what a horse you are!" He
was amused to find himself talking to his horse just
as Epifanio did during a horse breaking. Everybody
said he was like his uncle. After last night, he knew

he *felt* like Epifanio.

Epifanio always said it was better to take a chance with a hen than kill it to cure the pip. They'd been willing to take a chance with Marta and the stallion, and gained one thoroughbred. Martin felt that perhaps this was what it meant to be a gaucho, to do the best you could over the long haul and take a chance when you could without risking the herd. He knew now that he also put the herd first, but he blessed the gaucho who did come to care for Marta.

He was satisfied. If only he could reach the herd now so they would lose no more horses. The day of the gaucho was not over, for *he* was a gaucho.

"Mar-tin Gui-men-ez!" He shouted once above the morning wind and was content to let the sound sink into the pampa. It would not do to let his friends hear him bellow his name as if he were the domador.

The Bosque Alegre grew ahead like a dark green castle set in a sea of pampa grass. Did he see the thin swirling column of smoke from a fire? Martin spurred Gatito. That *must* be a fire. They were still there!

Now Gatito picked his way carefully between pine trees and bushes toward the sound and the smell of the herd. Martin watched for more smoke from a fire and sniffed for the faint smell of coffee. He noticed that Gatito's ears were forward and that he strained ahead even though he was drenched with sweat. He must be glad to be out of the valley of death and back with the herd.

They were deep in the forest now, and Martin slowed Gatito. He wanted to take his friends by surprise. Gatito carefully walked at the gait Martin ordered.

Martin peeked through the last trees and saw his uncle and friends sitting around the campfire. They were just finishing breakfast and looked comfortable after a good night's sleep. But he did not envy them. Carlos and Alonso might never spend a night alone with dying horses. Since he had saved Marta, he felt a night alone in the wilds was a magnificent ordeal.

"*Hola!*"

"Ah, Martin, finally!"

"We have been waiting for you," Epifanio said quietly.

"You're filthy as a pig!" Carlos said, and Martin realized he felt dirty. He must have soot all over himself from sticking so close to the fire last night.

"Well, a clean pig never gets fat," he retorted.

"Epifanio, doesn't it take a gaucho to have such wit after a sleepless night?" Carlos laughed.

"He is late. Perhaps he slept peacefully all night."

"How is Marta?"

"And the other, the stallion?"

"Wait a minute, please. I'm hungry and thirsty," begged Martin as he slid off his horse. He gave Gatito a slap on the rear, and the horse needed no further invitation to trot off toward the herd. Martin walked over to his uncle and held out his hand. Epifanio took it and held it in his own. Martin was aware that he stood a foot taller than the old gaucho.

"Marta will live, Domador," he said. He wanted to say more but could not.

"Good. Maybe she will be a champion one day— the golden mare with nine lives," Epifanio replied. He did not ask what had delayed his nephew.

"But the black stallion lies dead in the valley."

"He was dying as we left. You did well to save one."

Epifanio had actually said he did well. So that was what it took to merit praise from his uncle. Martin grinned broadly. Such praise was worth working for!

"I was beginning to worry about my harmonica, *amigo*. What kept you?" Alonso asked, finally.

"He was just worried that you might play better than he if you stayed away much longer," Carlos added, handing Martin galleta crackers and hot coffee. Martin accepted them gratefully. This was the first food he had eaten in twenty-four hours.

"No, it wasn't that I worried about competition. I was afraid he might charm the snakes and they would follow him."

"How long did the stallion live?" Epifanio cut into the teasing. He asked the question matter of factly. Martin stuffed the rest of the cracker into his mouth and swallowed. He shook his head, took a gulp of coffee, and finally spoke.

"I do not know, Domador. Till afternoon, I think.

I did not hear him stop breathing, but only gradually knew he did not live and that I was not surprised.

"About the gaucho who came to relieve me. His son broke a leg and he came as soon as he found a doctor—early this morning. I was almost ready to leave when he came," Martin added shyly.

Epifanio nodded and smiled. "Good," he said. "We could not ride without you."

"Carlos, I was so afraid all night. I saw snakes crawling toward me and pumas that were all eyes and vultures in the dead of night. And they were nothing but crickets in the grass! I was also afraid all the horses would die and leave me alone. Then I tried to work all the time so I couldn't think, and it helped."

"Ah—" Carlos started, but Epifanio waved him quiet so that Martin could go on with his story. He had not eaten or slept for a day and a night and his horse, already battered by the storm, had been bitten and lived, and the smell of dead horses still clung to his clothes. He had much to tell and his friends heard him in silence. Finally he told of the stumbling ride to reach the Bosque Alegre before they left.

"And it is a fortunate thing for me that you were all sitting by the fire telling tales like old women," he concluded with a grin.

"And that's the thanks we get for waiting here for this lazybones," Alonso groaned.

"You'll tell a passable tale yet," Epifanio said.

"So that is what a segundo does with his time? If

you should ever need a good lawyer, Segundo . . ." Carlos suggested.

"Carlos, don't be in such a hurry to get back to your books. They'll never be as exciting as this drive," Alonso told his brother.

"Tonight is our last night out, and we have the tourists with us, don't we?" Even Carlos sounded sad. He looked as if he were about to decide Alonso was right. He shrugged instead, and then asked, "But what happens when the drought is over? Won't we have to bring the horses back to Chepes again, to our ranch?"

Epifanio nodded, and all three boys brightened. This wasn't the absolute end of herding. "And you, Segundo, will you also be a lawyer with a fine clean office after last night?"

"I want to be a gaucho."

Epifanio stood looking at Martin for a long moment and then turned and walked over to his saddle-bags. He rummaged around until he pulled out a flat, cloth-wrapped package about fifteen inches long. Why was Epifanio carrying a thing like that on a drive like this? Martin saw that the package was carefully wrapped in oilcloth as Epifanio returned to the fire. He handed it to Martin, and his hands shook as he did so.

"Your father with his dying breath asked me to keep this for you until you become a man and had need of it," he said.

"*Gracias.*" Martin held the package without opening it. He had not known his father had left anything for him. He felt shy about opening it in front of his friends.

"Epifanio must have been waiting day and night for you to become a man," Carlos teased. "It is surprising that he hasn't given up hope, since the day of the gaucho is over."

Martin said nothing. Epifanio poured himself maté and sat down across the fire where he could watch his nephew.

"Come on, open it!" Carlos urged.

Martin grinned at Carlos, for he knew his friend could never wait for Christmas or his birthday. He nodded.

Gradually he stripped off the oilskin. Now he could feel what it must be, and he began to unwind the white cloth faster, with mounting excitement. He looked over at Epifanio with a questioning expression, and the old gaucho nodded his hawklike head. Yes, it could be nothing else. Finally he unwrapped some tissue paper.

A knife in its sheath, the whole about a foot long, lay in his lap. Both Martin and Carlos gasped, not because it was a knife, but because it was so intricately worked in silver and gold along both handle and sheath.

Slowly Martin pulled the knife from its sheath. First he tested it on some pampa grass, and it cut clean. Then he tried a small stick, and it cut clean. Finally he threw the knife at a tree, and it stuck deep in the trunk. He pulled the knife from the trunk, wiped it carefully, and stuck it back into the sheath. Martin neither said anything nor seemed aware of anyone.

"Well?" Epifanio said finally.

"I had nothing from my father, and I had only a short child's knife. And now, I have everything—almost. I will try to use this knife as my father would have," Martin told his uncle.

"What do you mean, you have *almost* everything?" Epifanio asked ominously. "What *else* do you need?"

"Martin, what a time to ask for favors." Carlos was astonished. "Now, of all times, when you should burst into tears of gratitude."

"What?" Epifanio repeated.

"Domador, you know that I am more than grateful. This is one of the great days of my whole life. But I worry about Marta. Now with my father's knife to protect me, could I not go back to the valley of death and care for her? The gaucho who is your friend cannot stay forever." Martin used every argument he could imagine to persuade Epifanio. The older man sat like a statue on a huge rock listening. He kept one eyebrow cocked skeptically. Finally he spoke into the silence that fell when Martin stopped speaking.

"When would you go?"

"After the drive is complete, after the horses are

in Calamuchita."

Epifanio heaved a sigh of relief. "I almost thought I had given you the knife too soon. But you have *some* sense of responsibility. *Bueno*—"

"May I go with him? Please?" Carlos surprised everyone, including himself, by asking.

"The lawyer?"

"I'll take some books."

"*After* the horses are safely in Calamuchita, then I will ask Don Jaime if he can spare you both for a few days to vacation with Marta. But now, *vamos*, eh? Don Jaime will be waiting." Epifanio got up and started to put out the fire.

"Thank you!" Martin said, grasping his uncle's arm.

"*Sí, sí, vamos!*" Talk was over. Epifanio was ready to leave.

"Just one more question," Alonso asked suddenly. "If my father cannot meet us because of some emergency or other, will his friend, Don Baudillo, still let us stay and pasture our horses, or will Martin have to use his new knife? If one of us has to fight, I volunteer," Alonso finished, standing militarily stiff and proud.

Epifanio laughed. His laugh echoed gaily through the forest. He could not seem to stop laughing. Finally he said, "*Gracias*, Patrón, but that will not be necessary—this time." Martin noticed that this was the first time Epifanio had not used the "cito" at the end of "patrón." Alonso was no longer the "little" boss. One day he would own the ranch, and Epifanio was pleased that he was willing to defend his birthright.

"You see, once a long while ago, I knew this friend of your father, this Don Baudillo. He was a poor gaucho like myself then, and we had ridden many a time together over the years. We had shared some adventures, Baudillo and I. But always we rode for other men over the endless pampa, for other men who grew fat on the land and realized great herds from the sweat of our bodies.

"Finally, we grew tired of sleeping on hard ground that was not always blanketed with stars. We were young and wanted wives and land and herds of our own. To keep the story short, for we must be on our way, we thought they lived well, these ranchers, and decided to join them.

"Neither of us was ever a man who could wait to own one horse and then another and another until at the end of his life he might have a dozen horses to will to as many sons. No, that was not for us. But neither were we thieves. You might say we had a problem, but, if so, the solution was right at hand.

"Now, if there was one man in all Argentina faster at throwing the boleadoras than me, well, I tell you straight out it was Baudillo. So on Sundays, after church, we would ride out where we were not known and frequent the places where men who already had tropillas of horses would gather.

"Baudillo and I each had one beautiful, pure black stallion. They'd been trained by Indian chiefs and were fast as the wind. We'd tell all takers that we were willing to match our skill with the boleadoras against theirs, our horses standing security.

"How they'd rush to the fray! Thinking us braggarts, you see, they'd bet the finest horse in their line. In this way we soon gained a fair herd, more than a hundred horses in less than a year. Good horses. The greater number were stallions, and blacks.

"All went well for a while. But perhaps we began to count ourselves great men too soon and did not watch our herd as closely as we should. It was hard to care for them well since we were still working for other men.

"To get to the point, the herd took sick. One day a mare developed a swelling inside the mouth that bulged her lips like balloons. We thought she'd been stung by a bee. Well, within a week the greater part of the herd was writhing in pain in the dust. The horses' mouths were so bloated the poor creatures couldn't swallow even a drop of water. They were dying like flies in the heat.

"And their cries were pitiful to hear! It seemed more than a man or a horse should bear. Baudillo nursed them well, going from horse to horse like a man possessed and rubbing each with a dozen salves, or so it seemed. He forced water and tea made from herbs of the pampa down each throat, though the devils bit him for his kindness as often as not.

"But it looked hopeless to me and I couldn't bear to see them dying and my friend most likely along with the last of them. You've smelled a dead horse?

"Then you'll understand when I say that one day I left with the dawn.

"*Amigo*, the horses are yours," I said and chose three healthy blacks from the lot and headed south. That night I slept under the stars and felt glad to be away from the stench and the responsibilty, too. I heard not a word of Baudillo for twenty years or more; and to tell the truth, when I thought of him it was with a sigh, for a good friend long dead.

"But one day we prepared a great asado for a distinguished rancher friend of your father, Alonso, and who should ride through the gate but my old friend, Baudillo. He's a grand rancher now and grown very fat in the years of his dignity. He's not thrown the boleadoras in a dozen years." Epifanio finished his tale.

"But don't you sometimes think what a rich man you might have been?" Alonso asked.

"Or a dead one. I have heard he has heart trouble and an ulcer of the stomach and takes twenty-three pills a day," Epifanio answered. "No, it is good to know when to ride away without looking back. Keeps a man in touch with his life. But this *Don* Baudillo will give us pasture without the use of your knife, I think." Epifanio raised one eyebrow, and laughed. They all laughed with him like conspirators.

"*Nos vamos, amigos*. On to Don Jaime!"

The three boys watched the wiry gaucho rush around the camp seeing that they were ready to ride. Today he wore his broad money-encrusted gaucho belt and his best black bombachas and white shirt. He had shaved himself for the first time during the trip. They thought he looked quite elegant and wondered how he managed, since *they* were still covered with the grime and dirt of eight days. Well, it was too late to change now.

They were breaking camp for the last time. Tomorrow would be more like a picnic than a serious drive, with all the amateur gauchos along for excitement. The four had shared and gone through a lot together these last days, and each hated to have it end. There would be many friends and other adventures but none ever quite like these.

Martin certainly did not want the drive to end. He was a gaucho now, and at the estancia he would be only a schoolboy. He kept remembering back through the trip. There was the storm and the puma and the knife fight. There was the feel of two hundred and more horses moving together through the wind of the high pampa. There was a simple thing like Epifanio reminding them that a gaucho must sleep with his head pointing in the direction he intended to ride in the morning or he would lose his way on the pampa.

Martin stuck his new knife savagely into his belt and mounted his horse. What did he think he was, daydreaming like a gossipy old hen? They were ready to ride!

"Huyiaaaaa!" Epifanio swung onto his great black horse and gave the cry that started the horses straggling to their feet. The three boys swung into action too, flashing their whips like a well-trained team, snapping them through the air, and yelling at the top of their lungs.

"Huyiaaaaa! Huyiaaaaa!" Gradually the proud Arabians clambered to their feet, rippling their muscles, arching their graceful necks, and looking reproachfully at the man and boys. Not already? Not again? There was food and water here? Why move on?

They were scrawny and weedy, carrying the dust of eight days' travel in their matted manes and tangled tails. There wasn't a horse without cuts and bruises, and many limped in the clear morning sunshine. Even colts and fillies bore deep scars in their dirty coats. But from the moment each tired horse stood up, there was no doubt he was a purebred Arabian!

Dust could not hide the grace of his conformation, nor the set of his neck and high flying tail, nor the long sensitive face, nor the flash of great eyes. Fatigue could not dull high spirits. They were worth the hardship and the struggle. They were worth fighting for!

This had been a long journey and a hard one for the horses, Martin thought, as they galloped over the pampa.

They'd lost fourteen horses and left one behind. But the horses stayed together now with an instinct they'd lacked in the beginning. Epifanio said that in ten days or two weeks they'd be as fat and sleek as ever. Martin had learned that if his uncle said something, it was going to happen. Epifanio thought like a man and reacted like an Arabian.

Suddenly the pace changed. They were in a clear plain now and Epifanio gave the word. "Gallop as you've never ridden before!"

"Give Don Jaime something to remember us by!"

"Show what they can do!"

Martin answered his uncle by urging Gatito, slapping his whip to the recado, and yelling his mightiest. Faster and faster they went. Onward! Faster! Faster!

Now they were galloping full tilt to the wind. Two hundred and thirty-five brave horses enclosed in a dust cocoon. How the earth rumbled! They'd hear them coming all the way to Calamuchita.

The horses were straining every muscle. Nostrils flared, mouths open, manes and tails flying. They were terrible in their strength and their speed, wild in their abandon, magnificent in their spirit!

Carlos saw the men first. They looked almost like a rock on the far horizon. Horsemen certainly. Don Jaime and ranch hands and friends. Men from the home ranch at Chepes who had come to hear how they had brought the horses through.

"Do you see them?"

"We made it! We made it!" Carlos shouted.

"Huyiaaaa!" Alonso cried, snapping his long whip in the air.

"*Hola!* They see us!" Martin yelled to the others.

"E-pi-fan-i-o!" bellowed the gaucho, louder than the horses, louder than the boys, echoing across the wide plains. A voice that matched the pampa.

Glossary

Arriba!—Hurry up!
asado—roast, barbecue
Basta!—Enough!
boleadoras—lariat with balls at one end which when
       thrown twist around animals' legs
bombachas—loose trousers, fastened at the bottom
bosque—forest
Bravo!—Hooray!
Buen suerte—Good luck
Buenas noches—Good night
Burro!—Stupid one!
Caramba!—Good gracious!
Caray!—Confound it!
casita—little house
chico—boy
doma—horse breaking
domador—horse breaker, tamer
estancia—ranch

facón—gaucho knife
galleta—Argentine bread
gaucho—Argentine cowboy, skilled horseman
Gracias—Thank you
Hasta mañana—Until tomorrow
Hasta la vista—Until we meet again
Hola!—Hello!
jacaranda—tall tropical tree with fragrant wood
loco—crazy, crazy one
magnifico—grand
manzanita—small apple
maté—herb tea
mesquite—a spiny shrub of Latin America
moro—a black horse
muchachos—lads
Muy bien—Very well
patrón—boss, landlord
patroncito—little boss
peso—about one penny
pobre—poor one
Qué cosa—How surprising
recado—message
segundo—assistant
siesta—nap
tropilla—string of horses
Vamos!—Let's go!
víbora de la cruz—poisonous snake with a cross on its
        head, similar to the coral snake
viscacha—burrowing rodent similar to the chinchilla